CW00358203

4809900009275 5

The Kansas Fast Gun

Dave Frome was a man with a secret past, which only a few friends knew. Holding himself responsible for the death of his family, he had vowed never to carry a gun again.

He wanted to be left alone to raise cattle on his Broken Arrow spread, but mining interests were in the hills, contaminating the water which brought life to Frome's cattle.

Hesta Le Roy, daughter of a neighbouring rancher, was horrified when Frome refused to carry a gun against the miners who had, she thought, killed her own brother.

It is not until he sees an innocent man brutally lynched that Frome buckles on his gun to battle with the bad men of both factions and eventually win the hand of the girl he loves.

The Kansas Fast Gun

ARTHUR KENT

A Black Horse Western

ROBERT HALE · LONDON

ISBN 978-0-7090-8794-6

Robert Hale Limited
Clerkenwell House
Clerkenwell Green
London EC1R 0HT

www.halebooks.com

Typeset by
Derek Doyle & Associates, Shaw Heath
Printed and bound in Great Britain by
CPI Antony Rowe, Chippenham and Eastbourne

CHAPTER 1

The sun was a ball of fire sinking behind the Broken Arrow Hills when Dave Frome pushed his bronc through scrub timber carpeting the slopes and through ravines which bubbled with water. As his pony splashed through belly deep he ran his fingers in the water, then put them to his lips. The tasting was unnecessary. The colouring, a rusty red, told him how heavily the water had been contaminated by copper.

The pony lunged up from the ravine, pushed through gaunt cottonwoods, and Frome saw a score of his Broken Arrow steers ahead, bunched by his ramrod, Matt Grape, and two of his crew.

They swung on seeing Frome, and pushed to meet him, faces hooded by grimness.

Grape leaned forward in his saddle. He spat, then inspected Frome's soaked denims, and said: 'Did you see the colour of that water, Dave?'

Frome said casually, 'I did better, I tasted it.'

His apparent lack of concern caused the three men to exchange glances.

Frome looked over the gather. They were poor steers.

'This all of 'em, Matt?'

The ramrod shrugged. 'Could be maybe fifty more scattered in the thickets.'

Frome said: 'Then I'd better comb these thickets with a couple of boys tomorrow.'

Grape smiled thinly. He was small, and looked insignificant and out of place in a saddle. But his face, tanned the colour of old leather, testified to the number of years he'd punched cattle. 'Could be too late tomorrow. Could be the miners will've helped themselves to what beef we've left up here. They've got to eat.'

Frome said softly: 'It'll have to be tomorrow. Nobody need risk a limb in these hills at night for a few scrubs.'

Grape shrugged, and changed the subject. He bent sideways in his saddle, holding on to the pommel, spat, then said, 'Lousy copper taste. Met a Double Star rider at noon. Told me Le Roy's plenty burnt up about these miners. Specially as the news is out that Peter Speakman's arriving to run things. He told me how there was a pow-wow last night at Le Roy's. All the ranchers were there, but you.'

Frome smiled suddenly. 'Now, Matt, you know I know about the conference Le Roy held. You know I got an invite. And you know I wasn't there because I'm not taking a hand in the starting of gunplay. With me siding them, they'd feel confident enough to tear these hills apart.'

Matt Grape said: 'You're the boss. I don't agree, but I only take orders.' He swung angrily on the two riders. 'What in hell are you two doing? Get these goddam steers shifted!'

The two men swung their ponies away.

'And don't, for Chris'sake, let them steers drink any of

6

that there copper poisoned water.'

Frome had been loose in the saddle, smiling, but suddenly his lips tightened and he balled his pony forward at one of the moving riders.

'Farrow!' he snarled. 'What's that tucked in your Levis belt?'

The boy turned, straightening his waistcoat with his elbow, trying to hide the tell-tale sheen of steel. He was unsuccessful, so he snarled, 'What does it look like, Mister Frome?'

Frome saw the bone grip of a single-action Colt. He said softly, 'You know my orders. Nobody carries a gun on my range.' He swung to Matt Grape. 'How come you allowed Farrow to tote a gun?'

Grape looked surprised. 'Didn't know he had it.'

Frome extended his hand. 'OK, Farrow, hand it over.'

The boy straightened in his saddle. His face was scarlet. 'By hell, I won't. I don't ride these miner-infested hills unarmed for nobody.'

Frome said, 'I gave you a chance, Farrow. You backed down. Be off my land in two hours. I'll send your pay to Plattsville.'

Farrow snarled, 'That's all I've been waiting for.' His hand snaked for the gun in his belt, and he spurred towards Frome, bringing up the gun to pistol-beat him.

Frome's arm snaked upwards. The leather quirt on his wrist snapped like a gun-shot. Farrow gave a little cry and the Colt span from his fingers. The rancher brought his pony skidding round. The two ponies cannoned into each other. Frome's fist came up and chopped at Farrow's jaw. It was all Farrow could do to keep his seat.

Frome jack-knifed down and scooped up the revolver,

then sent it spinning into a rock cluster. Without looking at Farrow again, he swung his pony through the herd. Farrow yelled, 'I'll get even with you, Frome,' but the rancher did not look round.

Frome had crossed the ravine when Matt Grape caught him up. The small man leaned sideways in the saddle, studying Frome with a mock intentness like a doctor with his patient. 'Hell, Dave, what's biting at your innards?'

Frome said, 'You know what.'

'Yeah, Dodge six years ago. But did you have to be so hard on Farrow? He's talking sense. You can't expect him to ride these hills gun-less.'

Frome snapped, 'I pay, I give the orders. Those who don't like it can drift.'

Grape scowled, 'You don't make sense. These miners will shortly be cutting down on any cowboy they see. You won't protect your men, and you're letting these sod-shifters destroy your land.'

Frome said, 'The miners won't shoot my boys. They know I'm not arming them.'

'Crap!' Grape growled. 'When this thing blows up, miners ain't going to look to see if a puncher's a Broken Arrow man before spitting lead at him. They can't see straight, any old how, they're burrowing in the dark most days.'

Frome snapped, 'How about getting the gather in?'

'When I'm good and ready,' Grape said. 'I'm just telling you that you can't fence-sit on this one. These hills are either for cows or for digging copper. Ain't room for both.'

'I'm not fence-sitting,' Frome said. 'I'm calling on Speakman as soon as he reaches Plattsville.'

8

'Chances are he won't see you, let alone take action about contaminating the streams. Only force talks to Speakman, and you don't pack a gun.'

Frome said, 'At least, I'm going to try.'

Grape swung his pony. 'OK, you're the boss.'

'So you keep telling me,' Frome smiled, 'but you're still arguing.'

'Isn't that what friends are for?' Grape grinned, and moved away.

The ramrod was halfway back to the stand of timber when the shot sounded. It was way off, buried and yet magnified by the hills. It could have been a mile away or it could have been three miles. There was no telling, for the hills twisted and distorted sound.

Frome quietened his spooking mount, his head cocked towards the hills. A minute passed, but no further shots followed.

Grape called, 'Hear that? It could've already started.'

Frome answered, 'And it could've been nothing more than a miner getting something for the pot.'

'Yeah,' Grape jeered, 'a Broken Arrow cow. Maybe the cattle are only scrubs up here, but they still wear your brand.'

Frome didn't answer. He watched his ramrod disappear through the timber, then forked his leg across his saddle horn. Water dripped, copper-red, from his damp trousers. He didn't notice it, busy with his thoughts and his Bull Durham bag.

When he had fashioned and lit a cigarette, he straightened in his saddle, his face lined with worry. Leathery wallowing sounds reached him from beyond the timber as the steers smacked down into the water-logged

9

ravines. Frome's gaze went on, climbing the timbered-slopes.

He wondered when it would end, and how. He wondered how much more stock he would need to shift. He wondered how long he could keep his temper if Speakman, as rumoured, extended his mining operations. Frome still had the fast-running Teap River uncontaminated by copper, but the Teap was fed from the hills. If that was contaminated, if he couldn't reach some sort of agreement with the mining company, then it was either put up, or shut up and get out.

And unless he could force a compromise, there would be a clash between the miners and the cow outfits. There wasn't enough water for both. It needed goodwill from both factions.

But could you compromise with Speakman? Speakman had to expand to satisfy his stockholders. That meant he would mine every ounce of copper possible. And ranchers like Glinton Le Roy, soon to be Frome's father-in-law, and the crippled Luke Benson, with Kyle Bennett ramroding for him, wouldn't tolerate that.

Broome, who managed the mines from Plattsville, had been willing to talk peace, but obviously Speakman was against that, otherwise he wouldn't be coming in to run things himself.

Frome thought of the shot he'd heard a moment ago, and it brought the old fear back to him. A memory, six years old, but as clear as on the day it happened, came to him.

His hands tightened on the saddle pommel as he remembered the meadow outside Dodge City. The acrid bite of cordite fumes hung sluggishly in the air. The bodies lay

10

side by side in the field around the dead horses.

Frome's father had died very quickly. But judging by the scattered cartridge cases, his three brothers had put up a fight, formed in a ring, pumping shells from carbines and handguns until the hammers clicked on empty magazines. Then they had fallen beneath the withering fire of shotgun, carbine and revolver.

It had been a carefully planned massacre, and Frome had sewn the seeds of that action when, two days before, he'd beaten a Stuart to the draw on Dodge's Front Street, and dropped him dying in the mud.

The dispute between the two families had started over a narrow slash of land which separated their properties.

A day after the ambush, when Frome had been laying plans for revenge, a smiling official of the Land Office drove up in a buckboard.

Neither the Stuarts nor the Fromes had title to the disputed land, he explained, because the Government held it. One day they would build a road there.

Frome had sold up and ridden out of Kansas an hour later. He hadn't carried a gun since.

CHAPTER 2

It was dark when Frome reached his home valley. Lamplight dripped from the windows of the bunkhouse, the cookshack, and his ranch cabin. As he came down the track and swung to the corral, the clatter of pots and pans told him Long Will was busy in the cookhouse.

Frome hesitated as he swung at the corral. He saw the paint pony tethered at the pole outside his cabin. The paint belonged to Hesta Le Roy. Normally, when she called, she stayed the evening, and would release the paint in the corral.

Frome unsaddled the pony, released it into the corral, and moved towards his cabin. Long Will saw him, however, and came hurrying from his kitchen.

'Miss Hesta's visiting, Dave,' he said, 'but she ain't aiming to stay long. And here's me baking a new-fangled pie. You two been a quarrelling?'

'No.'

'Well, you turn on that Kansas charm, son, and tell her about the new kind of apple pie I've cooked.'

Frome smiled, nodded. 'But there's nothing new about apple pie,' he added.

12

'Is about this one, Dave, I didn't use apples.'

Frome reached the cabin, stepped across the veranda and into the long room. A large logfire competed with a bolt lamp to light the room.

Frome knew where Hesta would be sitting, but he didn't look directly that way as he crossed the room to his bedroom, unbuttoning his shirt.

'Dave?' she said. He turned then. She was sitting on the hide settee before the fire, fingers lacing through her strawberry blonde curls, her long legs extended across the carpet, spurs inward so they wouldn't welt the carpet.

Frome smiled a greeting. The smile with which she'd welcomed him left her face. 'You weren't at the meeting?'

'No.' He hesitated at the door.

'You needn't kiss me until you have washed, Dave,' she said. 'I can't stand copper.'

He hid his hurt, moved into the bedroom, and stripped off his shirt. First Matt Grape, Farrow, and now Hesta, he thought grimly.

He reached the hand basin and poured water from the jug of still hot water Long Will had placed there. He was busy with the soap when she came across, looked at him, and stood by the door.

'I'm sorry, Dave,' she whispered, 'that wasn't a nice thing to say.'

'Skip it,' he said. 'So I wasn't at the meeting. So what went on, as if I couldn't guess?' He saw her stiffen, and he pushed it. 'Everybody talked violence. Chiswick said if he was thirty years younger he'd buckle on guns and ride like hell. And everybody said "Goddam it, where's Frome?"'

'All right, Dave,' she said softly, 'so you know your neighbours. And you're in the same kind of trouble.

13

Frankly I don't understand your position.'

'It's so very simple,' he said. 'You've heard it so many times. I don't want violence.'

There was a pause. Frome rinsed the soap from his face, arms and neck. Then she said, 'Tell me something, Dave. Tell me why there are no guns on this ranch?'

'On the rack behind you,' Frome said, 'you'll see four or five hunting rifles.'

'I don't mean toy guns.'

'No need for bigger guns,' Frome answered laconically, 'Indians haven't given trouble in fifteen years.'

'You're avoiding the question,' she said softly. She looked at him with puzzled eyes. 'Surely what Kyle Bennett said about you wasn't true?'

Frome smiled sardonically. 'I wouldn't know what he said, but I can make a shrewd guess.'

'All right,' she snapped, 'and the fact he labelled you coward doesn't worry you?'

Frome began to dry himself. 'Why should it worry me?'

She stamped her foot. 'How can you say that?'

He smiled. 'I am saying it. I can't go into action every time some two-bit gunslinger says something unkind about me.'

She flushed. 'Kyle Bennett isn't a two-bit gunslinger!'

Frome smiled. 'Sorry, I was forgetting he's your cousin and you were once almost engaged. But he's still small potatoes to me.'

'And what do you mean by that?'

'I mean that he and his crippled boss are one of a kind. I mean that when mavericks drift on to Luke Benson's Muleshoe lands, he and Kyle never run them back. I also suspect that they aren't slow in running off branded stock if the opportunity's right.'

'Nonsense!' she snorted.

Frome smiled. 'Did you defend me with equal vehemence when Kyle criticized me last night?'

She blushed. She said, 'I. . . . I didn't have to. Denny defended you.'

Frome smiled. 'Good for Denny. Your brother's the brightest of the bunch. He'll make a good boss for Double Star.'

She turned from the door then. She frowned, looked back, and said, 'Although we're engaged, Dave, I don't know a lot about you, do I? I know only vaguely where you came from, where you've been, what you've done.'

Frome buttoned a white shirt, moved to the door, and began to close it. 'It's a long story. One day I'll tell it to you. Now go and crack a whip behind Long Will, while I change.'

She smiled, nodded, and Frome closed the door.

While he changed, he pondered a problem. Only two people in the county knew of the incident at Dodge – Matt Grape and Sheriff Sam Justin. But Frome had never told Hesta, and now he wondered why he'd always drawn back at the very moment he was about to tell her. It seemed strange that he couldn't find the courage to tell the story to the girl he would shortly marry.

Hesta was halfway across the room to meet him when he came from the bedroom. 'Dave,' she said, 'Farrow's outside. Mad or drunk. He's threatening to kill you!'

Frome headed across the room and on to the veranda. He saw the boy in the glow of the light from the room. Farrow sat on a pony a yard from the step, a bottle of whiskey in one hand, a twenty-two sporting rifle in the other. He sent a stream of curses as Frome stepped forward.

Frome snapped, 'Button up, Farrow, there's a lady present.'

The boy swung, head jutting. 'Why, look at that, old yeller-belly telling me to button up. Now you look here, Mister Gun-Shy, I've got me a rabbit gun, and you'd better run and hide on account you're a rabbit.'

Frome said, 'You've got thirty seconds to ride, Farrow.'

'I'm going, Gun-Shy, and I ain't the only one. Nobody'll work for you much longer.' He saw Hesta in the doorway. 'Nor marry you, I reckon.'

'Right, you've said your piece. Now ride.'

Farrow grinned, brought the rifle up. He didn't finish the move. Frome lunged from the step and hit the pony in the side. The horse jack-knifed and came up on its forelegs, spilling the drunk from the saddle.

The spooked animal skidded away. Frome picked up the rifle, and began to jerk the cartridges from the magazine, spilling them on the ground. Then he threw the empty repeater into the brush, dragged the shaken Farrow up by his shirt front, and snapped, 'Start walking, Farrow. Don't let me find you on my land again.'

He pushed Farrow. The boy staggered back, regained balance, cursed loudly, then came at Frome, his fists chopping. Frome blocked two punches, taking them on the arm, and then he saw his chance and sent a right through Farrow's defence. There was a meaty smack as his fist connected on the point of the boy's chin, and Farrow folded.

Long Will came up. Men came spilling from the bunk-

16

house. The men looked sullen. There wasn't the usual laughter and talking which followed a fist-fight.

Frome said to the cook, 'Get Farrow to a bunk. When he comes round, put him on a gentle pony towards town.'

Frome returned to the cabin. Hesta Le Roy followed him, a question taking shape on her lips. Finally she said, 'Why did you hit him, Dave? He's a boy, and he's drunk.'

'Big enough to threaten me with a gun, though.'

She moved to face him. She said, 'Were you trying to prove something? Were you trying to show me how brave you were by knocking down a drunken boy?'

Frome turned away from her, crossed to a cabinet, and poured a whiskey.

CHAPTER 3

It was a thing you couldn't see, but Frome knew it was there, a silent, brittle barrier which had cut him completely off from the girl facing him across the table.

Long Will noticed it when he brought the dishes, and returned later with coffee to find his food uneaten.

Frome was fashioning a cigarette, seeking for some way to break the barrier, when he heard the hoofbeats. He got up, moved to the door, and the horsemen came galloping down into the valley, swinging in around the corral, and massing before his cabin.

Broken Arrow men came spilling from the bunkhouse. The combined lights of bunkhouse, cabin and cookshack shaped the men in the saddles. Sweat glistened on the flanks of their hard-ridden ponies.

A bulky man swung from a leading horse, and Frome recognized him as Glinton Le Roy. A tall slight man in dandified clothes dismounted next to him, and Frome recognized Kyle Bennett. A third man, also dismounting, was Frome's ramrod, Matt Grape.

Le Roy's voice was high. 'You seen Denny?' he said.

'Not for several days,' said Frome.

18

Le Roy grasped Frome's arm, and the rancher saw the worry which lined the old man's face. 'He rode off at sun-up, and he ain't back,' he stammered.

Frome was puzzled by the concern. Denny was a young man. He had wild oats to sow and there was a girl in a saloon at Plattsville that he was friendly with. But Le Roy's next remark brought a groan from Hesta and started Frome worrying.

Le Roy said, 'He went up to the Arrows again to spy on them miners. He knows it ain't safe to stay up there after sundown, and he's home well before dark.'

'But hell,' Frome began. He didn't finish it. Tightening his grasp on Frome's arm, Le Roy continued, 'And your boys, Dave, said they heard a shot in the hills. That right?'

'One shot,' Frome said. 'We figured a miner hunting some supper.'

'But don't you see it, Dave? Denny was up there at the mine. Them sonsofbitches found him, they'd plug him for sure.'

Frome knew that Le Roy was correct. 'His bronc probably went lame. That's rocky country. We'd better ride out and look for him. I'll saddle up.'

Kyle Bennett spoke for the first time. Frome saw the sneer on his fine-featured face. 'We'll need fresh broncs, too,' he said.

'How many?'

Bennett said sarcastically. 'Why, you can count, Dave. A round dozen for us. And then there's your boys.'

Frome hid his irritation. He didn't see why a dozen or more men were needed to look for Denny – especially in the treacherously rocky Arrows. 'Sorry, Kyle, but there isn't more than a half a dozen broncs in the corral.'

'Times like these,' Bennett said smoothly, 'a man should keep a score or more in the home corral.'

Before Frome could ask what Bennett meant by 'times like these', Matt Grape said, 'I'll take half the boys to the north meadow. There's thirty-forty broncs grazing there.'

Frome nodded to Matt, and the foreman swung away with half the men.

Le Roy followed Hesta into the cabin, but Kyle Bennett, rolling a cigarette, stopped by Frome on the veranda. He said silkily, 'I heard you call for a horse, but I didn't hear you call for a gun.'

Frome looked at Bennett through narrowed eyes. He didn't like what he saw. Bennett was a dandy with a quick gun. Blond of hair, too handsome and grey of eye. His reputation as lady-killer was only second to that of gun duellist. They said Bennett was the fastest gun in the county, but Frome didn't agree. He knew somebody who was faster.

Frome said, 'That's right, I didn't call for a gun.'

Bennett smiled thinly, but before he could reply, Le Roy had stepped back on to the veranda. The old rancher stopped before Frome, the man who would be his son-in-law. 'I didn't want him going up there, Dave, honest I didn't.'

Bennett said, 'Don't blame yourself, Glinton. Pity there aren't more with Denny's guts in this county.'

Frome said, 'What did he expect to find out which he couldn't have got from a drunken miner in town for the price of a drink? Whose idea was it to send him up there?' He felt the anger boil within him. He swung at Bennett. 'Was it your idea?'

Bennett avoided an answer. Looking at Le Roy, he

snapped, 'If they've harmed him, they'll get hell. We'll string 'em up, even it it takes us a year.'

'Mighty big talk, Kyle,' Frome said softly.

Bennett stiffened. The palms of his hands rubbed against the pearl-handled grips of his pair of six-guns. It was as if his palms itched.

Long Will came across from the corral. 'Horses are ready!'

Frome led the way to the corral and swung aboard a paint pony, turning it into the press of riders. A yard away, Bennett stepped into a saddle, then bent to talk to a Broken Arrow cowboy. His words reached Frome. 'Ain't you Broken Arrow boys riding?' he asked.

'Isn't enough broncs, Mister Bennett,' came the answer. 'Besides, we ain't allowed to pack guns.'

Bennett sneered. 'High time you boys joined a good outfit. If war comes, I'll be hiring boys at gun wages for Luke Benson. Spread the word, won't you?'

The Broken Arrow man said eagerly, 'I sure will, Mister Bennett.'

Frome pushed the paint through the press, stringing out into the lead, swinging up the valley track, then heading across prairie towards the Arrows, which towered black triangles beneath a curtain of stars.

Hesta Le Roy, standing besides Long Will, heard the riders go, her knuckles showed white as she gripped the rail. 'It isn't true, is it, Will?' she asked.

'Ma'am?'

'That Dave's a coward?'

Long Will mumbled, 'I don't rightly know the answer to that.' He hobbled quickly across to the cookshack.

*

21

They crossed the grasslands, crashed through timber, swung along a series of hogbacked ridges which reared up from the ground like blisters and thundered across the rock-strewn approach to the Lone Pine Canyon.

Le Roy called a halt at the bottle-neck mouth, and stood up in his stirrups. A lone horseman swung from a stand of timber. 'That you, Mister Le Roy?'

'Any sign of my boy?' Le Roy snapped.

Frome saw the silhouette of rider, horse and carbine cradled in his arms. 'Nobody's come out, Mister Le Roy,' he said.

Bennett said, 'There's only one other way. The Plattsville Road. But even if he crossed the hills, Denny wouldn't take it. Too many shovel-heads use it.'

Le Roy's voice broke as he ordered the lone rider to take them to the spot from which Denny Le Roy had watched the mining camp.

They swung down into the canyon, using its rim to guide them for the moon had not yet appeared. They crossed the scrub-grown basin, the beat of hoofs cannoning from the tall canyon walls. They veered left, then began to climb. The only sounds were the bite of steel-shod hoofs on stone, the hard breathing of men and horses and the curses of the men as the horses slid on the loose shale.

The track narrowed and the leader advised Le Roy to continue on foot. They left the horses and moved up the steepening track in single file.

Then the leader stopped, struck a match, and indicated a six-foot wide crevice. 'Denny would keep his bronc here.'

Bennett entered the crevice, striking a match, and reappeared a minute later. 'Nobody there now, but there's recent horse droppings.'

They moved on, and Frome noticed that Bennett was hefting his carbine.

The climb became steeper. Panting and sweating, they reached a flat, disc-shaped plateau, and moved across it to its furthest edge, and the leader pointed over the edge. 'Denny watched from here. Look over, and you can see the miners' camp and the diggings.'

They bent to the rim and looked down on the silent camp. A few campfires burnt, a man was singing, nothing else. Suddenly the leader jerked them around, his voice edged with hysteria. 'Mister Le Roy, there's fresh blood in this hollow.'

Frome, Le Roy and Bennett moved into the hollow. Bennett struck a match. They saw the five-inch blood stain on the polished surface of the rock. Frome thought of the shot he'd heard that evening; Le Roy groaned; Bennett touched the pool with a finger. 'That's a lot of blood,' he said grimly.

A voice reached them from across the canyon. A challenge. Bennett dropped the match, smashing his boot on it. The voice came again, and the hills took up the sound and turned it into a series of echoes.

There was a metallic smack as if a rifle barrel had hit rock. Bennett snapped, 'Mine sentry,' and brought his carbine up. Le Roy dragged the gun down. 'Don't fire, Kyle. They might have my boy.'

The warning came once more. The men didn't move. Then the shot came. Flame stabbed across the plateau from the adjoining hill. A slug skidded across rimrock with a screeching sound. Men dropped; Bennett cursed and snatched the rifle from Le Roy's grasp. He aimed at the

23

point of the rifle flash, and fired.

Le Roy snapped: 'You fool! Let's get out of here. Think of my boy!'

They scrambled from the hollow and flooded back across the plateau. Two more shots cracked out from the sentry. They slipped and slid down the narrow track and reached the horses. Bennett snapped, 'Let's get our carbines, get back there, and give them hell.'

'They might have my boy alive,' Le Roy said. 'Let's ride. We'll send Sheriff Justin in tomorrow.'

They mounted and turned down track. It was easier going for the moon was up. They hit the canyon floor, and put their reluctant ponies into a gallop. It was Kyle Bennett who brought them to a halt with a shout. His arm jack-knifed towards the lone pine from which the canyon took its name. 'What's wrong with the old pine? Looks as if it's sprouted a new trunk.'

Fear raced along Frome's spine. 'That's no trunk,' he said savagely, 'that's human. Somebody's been hanged there!'

They swung and quirted and spurred new life into their spent animals. They covered ground fast, lashing the animals, and reached the wall in a ragged line. Frome and Bennett stepped from saddles on to a track and scrambled to the rim. They reached the pine and Frome swung the stiffening body. He looked up into the twisted features of Denny Le Roy.

From across the canyon floor, there came the drum of hoofs. Matt Grape was bringing up the rest of the boys.

CHAPTER 4

They sat ponies in a circle. Denny lay beneath a shroud of slickers on a shelf of rock. Several men held torches of corded grass. Glinton Le Roy silently looked down at his son.

A horse pawed at the stone floor. Flame sizzled through damp grass. A horse snorted. There were no other sounds. Frome watched Le Roy, and Bennett. Anger against Bennett was a hard core in his throat. He felt certain that it was Bennett who had persuaded Denny to spy on the miners' camp. And what had Denny hoped to find out? He could have bribed a shovel-head in Plattsville for as much information as was obtainable from looking down at the camp from the rimrock.

Frome swung his pony and leaned towards Matt Grape. 'Matt, go fetch Sam Justin,' he whispered.

Bennett heard him. He snarled, 'We don't want the sheriff!'

Frome said, 'This is murder. Sam's to be told.'

Bennett sneered, 'We'll tell him a month from now. This is our business. We'll handle it.'

Frome turned to Le Roy. 'It's what Glinton says that counts.'

Bennett swung to Le Roy. 'What do we do, Glinton? Do we tell that mine-loving sheriff, or do we handle this ourselves?'

Frome snapped, 'Watch it, Bennett, Sam's a friend of mine.'

'First thing we bury Denny,' Le Roy said; 'then we ride after the sonsofbitches who murdered him.'

Frome bent forward. 'Glinton, leave it for Sam.'

Le Roy was against it, Frome knew that. The old man wouldn't answer him directly.

'If Sam says ride against the miners, that's OK. But he's got to know,' Frome said.

Le Roy said: 'I'm not saying a word against Sam. But he'll need proof. If he gets it, them mine companies have slick lawyers. He'll never get a court conviction, Dave. We'll handle this in our way.'

Frome said grimly, 'I'm sending word to Justin.' He swung at Matt Grape. 'I gave you an order, Matt.'

The ramrod hesitated, torn between conflicting loyalties – his loyalty to his friend and to the cattlemen.

Le Roy moved towards Matt Grape. 'Before you ever worked for Dave, you were a cattleman, Matt. You know it won't be any good bringing in the sheriff. You also know what these miners are up to. Dave's upset. He'll see it our way at daybreak.'

Grape looked unhappy, looking first at Frome and then at Le Roy.

Frome said, 'Matt, in this matter follow your own conscience. If you don't ride for Sam, I won't hold it against you.'

Grape extended a pleading hand. 'I don't figure it wise to tell Sam, Dave. Anyhow, he can't get out here until daylight.'

Le Roy swung towards Kyle Bennett. 'Spread the word, Kyle, that I'm hiring guns. I'm paying eighty a month, and I'm providing new guns and blooded horses.'

'Right!' Bennett swung to the mounted men. 'Three-four of you ride across the county and spread the word.' He sneered. 'And don't overlook the bunkhouse at the Broken Arrow.' He turned to Matt Grape. 'I'm sure Luke Benson would like you to ride with us, Matt.'

Grape pondered that. He looked at Frome.

Frome said, 'You're a free agent in this matter, Matt.'

Grape said, 'Thanks for the offer, Kyle, but I'd prefer to ride for Glinton's outfit, if he'll have me.'

Le Roy said, 'Glad to have you, Matt. You can ramrod a new crew.' He hesitated. 'You can also carry out a tough job for me, Matt. Ride to the Double Star. Tell my wife . . . Hesta.'

Grape only nodded, and backed his pony away, turning along the edge of the canyon. Four men swung after him to carry out Kyle Bennett's instructions of gathering men.

Le Roy turned away from the slab of stone on which his son rested. He stepped into his saddle, and turned to Bennett. 'You're the only male kin, I have. I'd like you to forget our differences in the past, Kyle, and come back to ramrod for me?'

'I'll check with Luke,' Bennett said. 'He won't object. Thanks, Glinton.'

Le Roy said: 'This is what I want you to do at sun-up. Take a buckboard and escort to Plattsville and fetch a case of those new sixty-sixty Winchesters from Gulick's store. Bring plenty of ammunition. Also a couple of dozen Colts with shellbelts.'

A rider nearby snapped, 'Somebody's coming!'

They swung, looking across the canyon floor.

Another rider said: 'Can't see him, but can hear him. He's singing.'

A voice reached Frome, distant yet recognizable. A man singing.

Le Roy said, 'Let's look into it.'

They swung and spurred across the floor, spreading out then curving in towards the lone rider they eventually saw in the canyon's centre. Long before they reached him, the man had stopped, peering forward anxiously from the back of his pony. They slackened speed, closed in on the man and ringed him.

The man looked from one gaunt-visored cowpuncher to another, and, frightened by their silence, he stuttered, 'What – what is it?'

Bennett said: 'Who are you?'

'Me?' the man relaxed. 'Name's Tony Wolf. Been on a drunk. Had a dandy time.'

'And what are you doing in the canyon this late?' Bennett asked.

'Going home.' Wolf didn't like Bennett's tone of voice.

'Where's home, under a goddam rock?'

Wolf stiffened. 'The mine – I work at the mine.'

'Funny way to get to the mine. Difficult for a sober man at night, let alone a drunk.'

Wolf shrugged. 'I knew I shouldn't have come this way. But I was drunker than I am now. It seemed a good idea an hour ago.'

Bennett moved his pony forward. He bent, his voice low. 'I think you're lying, Wolf. I think you came back here to see if the fruit you'd hung on the lone pine was there.'

'Fruit?' Wolf said. 'What's this about?'

'The boy you found spying on the mine – remember? You shot him, then you hanged him on the pine. Then you went on a drunk to town, and returned to admire your handiwork.'

Tony Wolf stiffened. He swung his pony. But Bennett slammed forward. His quirt flaked out and the leather thonging curled round the miner's body with a cracking sound.

The cowpunchers on either side of Frome balled their ponies towards the miner, reaching for their revolvers.

'Tell the truth!' Bennett screamed.

Frome's movements were reflex. A poor drunk was in trouble and he acted. Spurs lashed the paint's flanks, the pony bounced between Bennett and the miner, and Frome snatched to free the thonging. 'Lay off, Bennett!' he snarled.

'Keep out of this, Frome!' Bennett cried. His hand sank to his gun. 'Or by hell, I'll cut you down!'

Frome had the thonging of the quirt in his hand. He snatched it downwards suddenly, jerking Bennett's hand away from his gun.

Bennett shouted, 'We're going to lynch this miner, and nobody's going to stop us.'

'You're not,' Frome said, 'and I'll see that you're not.'

'They lynched Denny, didn't they?' Bennett snarled.

'Maybe. But this sod-shifter says he was in town. I believe him. He's innocent, so he goes free.'

'Denny was innocent. Look what they did to him.' He swung, looking back for Le Roy. 'Let Glinton decide,' he snapped. 'What do we do, Glinton?'

There was a tense moment of silence. Frome looked from one grimly-set face to another, but saw no hope

29

there. Le Roy suddenly swung his pony from the circle. 'What do we do, Glinton?' Bennett shouted again.

Le Roy's answer was loud and clear and precise. 'Do like he did to my boy.'

Frome snapped, 'Glinton, wait!' But it was too late. The cowpunchers closed in, boring their broncs at the miner, eagerly reaching for him to tear him from his saddle. Bennett's pony cannoned into Frome's. Stirrup to stirrup, elbow to elbow, Frome tried to keep him from Wolf.

'For the last time, Frome . . . you with us or against us?' Frome saw Bennett's sweating face inches from him.

'Harm Wolf,' he snarled, 'and I'll come gunning for you.'

Bennett's mouth was tight against his teeth. 'Now I'm worried,' he gritted.

Cowpunchers closed in on Wolf from the other side. A fist hammered at the miner's face and blood gleamed there. Frome made one last desperate effort to save him. Viciously spurring the paint away from Bennett, he lashed at the bunched riders. A man yelled as the paint caught his pony broadside, sending it crashing. A head reared suddenly before Frome, and he slammed at it. The head disappeared below him.

Frome swung the pony, bringing it around the miner's, striving to clear a path. He freed his foot from the stirrup and kicked at a man. He caught another with his quirt, sending the man twisting from his saddle, hands to face, screaming with pain.

He came alongside Wolf and saw Bennett closing in. Bennett was cursing. Frome reached for the headstraps of the miner's mount and simultaneously lashed the paint with his spurs, trying to break from the melee and drag the miner with him.

But stirrup irons grazed his legs. Then a horse crashed into the paint. There was a loud report, like the snapping of bone, and the paint began to fold beneath him. Frome came up, clawing at Bennett's pony, trying to drag it down. Then something cracked across his forehead and his head seemed to explode. Vomit clogged his throat. He snatched for Bennett's saddle pommel, determined to get Bennett.

The only sound was a shriek, followed by the curses of men and the pain cry of horses.

Then something cracked down across his skull, and he felt himself sinking into a suffocating darkness.

CHAPTER 5

It hurt. It felt as if somebody had put a bucket on his head and was beating it. He knew that he was sitting up and knew that somebody was holding him there. Red hot flames seemed to dance before his eyes, he groaned, and the arms eased him down on his back again, and the pain eased.

Water trickled across his face, and a voice reached him. 'Look now,' it said. He looked. Somebody was shielding his eyes with a grey, sweat-stained hat. You never saw Matt Grape without it. He recognized Grape's voice now.

'How do you feel, Dave?'

'Terrible, but it can't last.'

'Somebody sure hit you. Slight concussion. But you'll mend.'

Memory came back, and Frome moved, lifting, opening his eyes, ignoring the sharp pain. First he saw the dead paint pony. It lay a yard from him, its head twisted, neck broken. Frome brushed Grape's hat away, looking to the canyon rim through the sun-dazzle.

Grape said softly. 'Wolf's up there, Dave.'

Frome folded back, groaned, bunched his fists. 'Bennett,' he said, 'I've got to get Bennett.'

Grape poked a flat bottle at him. 'Whiskey. Drink this, Dave. It's good to hear you talk like that again. I've been waiting to hear a man-sized emotion from you for six years. Now you're going to strap on a gun, go for Bennett, and that's a good thing, no matter what the outcome.'

Frome took a long pull at the bottle and shook his head. Grape said, 'Bennett'll do for a start. Always thought he'd lived too long.'

Frome said, 'What do you mean – for a start?'

'Well, once you've dropped Bennett and shown the county that you're a man, you can clean up this mess. The word's that Speakman's brought gunhawks with him.'

Frome snapped, 'Not interested. I'm after Bennett. Bennett lynched Wolf. Without him, it wouldn't have happened.'

Grape said: 'Bennett can't carry all the blame for that. Nor the mining company. You carry a load of the blame.'

'Me!' Frome came forward, winced, then relaxed, 'How do you figure that?'

'I'm dealing with fundamentals,' Grape said. 'You've been playing half-man for years. Don't you think that if you'd been yourself Le Roy and the others would've ignored you? If you'd been yourself, they would've listened to you – not Bennett. They only listened to him because he's the only one who shows any guts and leadership around here.'

Frome took an angry pull at the bottle. 'For an old ranny, your reasoning astonishes me, Matt.'

'Maybe, but I'll push it further. If you'd shown yourself a man, Denny wouldn't be dead. He died because he listened to Bennett. He looked up to you, but you deserted him. You would've stopped him from doing anything stupid like spying on the mine.'

Frome snapped, 'You're confusing the issue. I'm after Bennett, the rest doesn't matter. With Bennett out of the way, this business will fizzle out and get settled over a conference table.'

He swung up, shook his head. The pain was still there, but the whiskey neutralized it. He took another drink, then looked about him. He saw the lone pine and the body away in the distance, almost invisible in the sun glaze. He saw two ponies tethered to brush near at hand. He extended his hand, palm upwards. 'All right, Matt, I'll take that Le Roy gun-belt you're wearing.'

Grape made no protest. He began to unbuckle it. 'Glinton won't like you gunning his nephew.'

'Glinton'll get over it. He isn't all that fond of Kyle.'

'Maybe. Before he lost his son. Kyle's his only blood male relative. Blood talks.'

'More of your goddam fundamentals, Matt.' Frome took the shell-belt and holster Grape handed him, buckled it around his waist, then got painfully to his feet. He stood straddle-footed for a moment, swaying, shaking his head.

He dusted his clothes, straightened the holster on his hip, and moved carefully towards the horses.

Grape said, 'Pain gone?'

'Nope, but I can carry it.' He brought the Colt from the holster, checked the load, dropped it back into leather. 'You don't work for me, Matt, but you can do me another favour. Bury Tony Wolf. Better do it tonight.'

Grape nodded, followed him to the horses. 'Where are you heading now, Dave?'

Frome selected the fastest horse, a big black. Both

carried the Double Star brand. 'To showdown with Bennett. You'd better not follow me too closely. I don't want you involved.'

He swung aboard the black, jacked it round, and used the spurs.

Matt Grape watched him go. He smiled. After six long years, he thought, Dave Frome was a man again.

Frome reached the Double Star headquarters a little after high noon. He came over a ridge and saw the sprawling ranchhouse, bunkhouse, barns, stables and corral laid out before him, white in the heat. Smoke was reefing up from the cabin and cookhouse chimneys, and it wasn't hard for Frome to see why. Both kitchens were pumping out victuals for the new men who were riding in.

Frome could see that the corrals were packed with ponies. The overdraft were hitched to the poles outside. Now he could see men, talking in groups or stretched in the shade provided by the buildings.

Frome put the black down the hill and cantered round the corral five minutes later. He had been spotted way out, and his coming had caused excitement. The word must have reached the ranch cabin, but neither Le Roy, Bennett nor Hesta came on to the stoop.

The silence was brittle when Frome put the black to the corral, tethered it, and stepped away. He knew the majority of the men who stood about the yard, but none saluted him. They ignored him.

Frome stepped towards the house, and three punchers talking in the way, shifted. Frome jabbed a finger at one of them. 'You, go tell Kyle Bennett to step out. With his guns on.'

The man swallowed and stumbled towards the house. Frome watched him disappear through the door, and began to move again, his big body bent slightly forward, his fingers just away from the holstered gun.

A moment later Glinton Le Roy, looking older, came on to the veranda. Hesta, dressed in a crisp black frock, followed him, looking at Frome coldly.

'Where's the dandy?' Frome snapped at them.

Le Roy looked glumly at his daughter, not knowing how to handle the situation. Hesta snapped, 'Fortunately for you, Kyle's away. Now go home before you make a fool of yourself.'

The fact that Hesta was addressing him as a little boy or a coward, only made Frome more angry. 'I'll wait for him,' he snapped.

Le Roy said, 'Do like Hesta says, Dave. Go home, sleep it off. You don't want to tangle with Kyle. He's fast.'

A voice, purposely disguised, came from a bunch of cowpunchers. 'You look out up there, there's a gunfighter a facing youse.'

Men began to laugh. Frome did not look back. 'I remember. Kyle's gone to collect some guns from Gulick. He shouldn't be long. I can wait.'

There came a movement from behind Frome. A furtive movement. He crouched, listening, ready to spin. He looked quickly at Le Roy and Hesta and saw them stiffen.

A harsh voice came at Frome. 'You've got a quarrel with Kyle, mister. I can act proxy for him.'

'Isn't no call for you to interfere, Talbot,' Le Roy snapped. 'Dave's just going.'

Frome smiled. That would be Martin Talbot. Another gun-slinger. A no-good, a bully, a cheat. It seemed Bennett was getting together a real rough crew. He reflected that while he was waiting for Bennett, he could thin out the man's friends. Without turning, he snapped, 'Talbot. I've heard your name. If it's Martin Talbot, I've heard nothing nice about you.'

'Say what you like,' the man said softly, 'but after I kill you I'll still weep a little.'

Hesta moved on the veranda. 'Talbot! Return to the bunkhouse!' She looked pale and scared.

'Sorry, ma'am,' Talbot said. 'Frome's insulted me.'

Frome, still facing Hesta and Le Roy, and with Talbot directly behind him, smiled. He knew Talbot wanted to nail him now; and he felt the old, almost forgotten thrill, of pending battle.

'You'd better turn, Frome, you're important in these parts. I want to see an important man die.'

Frome turned smoothly, dropping into his crouch, legs spread. He saw Talbot thirty paces away. Talbot was big, hulking, bearded, with a large slab face and a dropped right shoulder, the product of long handgun practice. Talbot's gun was low on his thigh in a tied-down holster. His hand, fingers splayed, was only inches from the butt. 'You get first call, Frome,' he said casually.

Hesta snapped from behind Frome. 'This foolishness must stop!' He heard her moving across the boards. Seeing that the Le Roys were moving to interfere, and anxious to get Frome, Talbot dived for his gun.

It was his last move. He was quick, but not quick enough. His gun was only half clear of leather, when Frome's slug took him between the eyes. He staggered forward, his gun slipping back into leather. His leg came up as he tried to keep erect, and then he thundered to the ground, falling on his face, his fingers clawing at the dust.

Frome slotted the gun. He turned to the Le Roys. He saw their surprise and it made him smile. 'Second thoughts. I won't wait for Kyle. I'll call on him in a day or two when he's had time to reflect and practice a little. After all, Talbot was a fast gun.'

He turned, moved along the corral. Men stepped hurriedly aside. Finally he found what he was looking for, a bronc carrying a Broken Arrow brand. He didn't want to be beholden to the Double Star for anything.

Swinging aboard one of his own ponies, he rode out of the yard without looking back.

CHAPTER 6

Dave Frome, wedged in at the long polished bar of The Drovers saloon, pushed his glass across the counter, and said to Mike Sturmer, 'Fill it, Mike.'

The bar was packed to overflow. Plattsville had changed in the few short years Frome had known it. The railhead had followed the mining companies; Plattsville had mushroomed into a score of streets and alleys. There were a dozen bars and honkytonks on Main alone. Every one would be packed, mainly with miners, citizens and a few cowpunchers.

Mike Sturmer pushed a fresh beer across the bar. He looked at Frome thoughtfully. He thought that the rancher was drinking too much, was too silent, had troubles.

Frome built a cigarette. The excitement of the gunfight had worn off and left him depressed. Hesta's welcome had been definitely hostile, and he wondered if it was all over between them. Of course, Hesta had lost her brother . . . but even so her welcome had been unfriendly.

Could it be Kyle Bennett, he wondered. Kyle and Hesta had been very close once when the man had ramrodded for Le Roy. There had been an understanding between them. But then Hesta had found that Kyle had been marking time with a half-breed girl in Denton beyond the Arrows. Come to think of it, Frome reflected, Bennett still spent a lot of time Denton way.

When Hesta had discovered the other woman, Kyle Bennett had left the Double Star and joined Luke Benson at the Muleshoe. Benson was a permanent cripple following a fall from a horse, and had been glad to hire Bennett to manage his spread. And now Kyle was back to the Double Star . . . and to Hesta?

And Frome had another worry. Matt Grape with his fundamentals, as he always called them, seemed to have hit on the truth out at the Lone Pine Canyon when he'd said that Frome was partly responsible for the deaths of Denny and Wolf. Frome wondered if he had been right in discarding guns after the Dodge tragedy. He thought he was; he thought violence was useless, never solved anything . . . but then there were people who could only be held in by violence.

Frome was about to lick down the cigarette paper, when somebody jogged his arm, and the fine shreds of tobacco spilled from the paper. He swung and saw the girl.

'I'm terribly sorry,' she said.

Frome grinned. 'It's all right. Too many packing this bar, anyhow.' He put pressure on a group of miners standing to his right so that the girl could reach the bar.

She smiled. 'Thank you.'

Frome liked the sound of her voice. She was dark, attractive, and lacked that brittle hardness he associated with saloon girls. She wore a long dark cloak and Frome could see the glittering sequins of her stage costume through the front of it. Aware suddenly of Frome's interest, she closed the gap. She reached the bar, bent forward, and signalled Mike Sturmer.

Sturmer came along the bar. 'Did you want me, Curly?'

'I'm going to dinner, Mike.'

Sturmer frowned. 'It's busy in town tonight. Don't you think it'd be safer if you ate in your room? I'll have something sent up.'

'Look, Mike,' the girl said firmly, 'I'm tired of eating in my room. I'm only going next door.'

Sturmer said. 'But we're busy, kid. I can't spare anybody to escort you. There's a rough crowd in town. And you're quite a hit. Most people've heard you sing. You might be pestered.'

Frome said, 'I can always escort the little lady, Mike. I haven't heard her sing, so she hasn't affected my reason.'

Sturmer smiled, the girl looked uncertain. 'Why not? You've been sitting at this bar all evening, Dave. You need cheering up.' He turned to the girl. 'Mister Frome will escort you, Curly, if it's OK with you.'

The girl looked at Frome, then at Mike Sturmer. 'If you say so, Mike, I have no objections.' She smiled at the rancher. 'I'll be happy to accept your invitation.'

Sturmer said quickly, because people were waiting to be served, 'I'd better introduce you. Curly, meet Dave Frome; Dave, meet Curly.'

Frome touched his hat.

They left the packed bar and turned left on the board-walk. The girl took Frome's arm. They crossed the alley to the restaurant, entered it. Frome was surprised that he was a little unsteady on his feet and light-headed. He put it down to a lack of food and sleep.

41

The girl sat opposite Frome and, in the better lighting of the restaurant, he could see that she was indeed beautiful. Her skin was smooth and softly sun-tanned, her eyes large and intelligent, her hair glossy black and curled. Frome reflected that here was no saloon girl. He remembered then that Sturmer had said she was a singer, and recalled hearing that Sturmer's business had so increased that he was hiring featured players from the bigger towns and had built a stage at the rear of the saloon.

They made small talk. Frome asked the girl how she liked the town, and she said she liked it. She asked Frome what line of business he was in, and he said cattle, and she said she had lived on a ranch once.

The waitress arrived and asked Frome what he would like. Frome said, 'Ask the lady first, please.'

The girl ordered; Frome said he would have the same; and the waitress left.

Curly said, 'Thank you, Mister Frome.'

'For what?'

'For treating me as a lady.'

'Aren't you?' Frome smiled.

She shrugged. 'A lot of people don't think so. No matter how you live, if you're on the stage. . . .'

Frome said, 'The waitress didn't mean anything. She knows me. I leave a large tip. Besides, she's jealous. You're pretty, Curly.' He smiled. 'Very pretty.'

She lowered her head. She was smiling. 'You've had a little too much to drink. Mister Frome.'

'It's not that at all,' Frome said. 'There's something about you, Curly . . . all of a sudden I've forgot my troubles.'

She said, still smiling, 'Mike Sturmer was right. I should've stayed in my room. This town isn't safe. I'd better get back to The Drovers. . . .'

'Without any dinner?' Frome smiled.

'Oh, I must eat. And I'm sure I'm safe. Mike wouldn't have agreed otherwise.'

'I've known Mike six years,' Frome said, 'I've never known him to make a mistake. But there's always a first time.'

She smiled broadly then. 'I'll take that chance, Mister Frome.'

Frome heard footsteps behind him, but he did not look round. A hand touched his shoulder. He swung, hand sinking to the Colt in the cutaway holster. He saw Sam Justin looking down at him. The sheriff was redheaded, barrel-chested, in his early fifties, but had the capacity for hard-riding and desk work of a much younger man.

Frome's hand slid back to the table. 'You're the man I've been trying to avoid, Sam.'

'It figures,' Justin said heavily. 'You're packing a gun, and you look beaten-up. Don't tell me a buffalo kicked you in the head.'

Curly looked from the sheriff to Frome, puzzled, a little anxious.

'Never known you to hit town without calling in to see me,' Justin said. 'What's the matter – guilty conscience? Something happened I ought to know about?'

He reached for a chair, swung it to face the rancher, sank his big frame on to it. Frome was smiling at him, and he didn't like that. 'I see the gun on your belt. Unusual to see you carrying one?' he prompted.

'We all change, Sam.'

43

'That's a fact,' Justin said flatly. 'I see Bennett's changed – back riding for Glinton. Isn't that odd?' He saw Frome's lips tighten slightly. 'Saw him in Gulick's this morning, buying rifles for Glinton. I asked myself why Glinton wants all those guns.'

'Did you find an answer?'

'Naturally. But you haven't told me about those head bruises. Buffalo?'

Frome said easily, 'Now, Sam, if I said "buffalo", you'd say there ain't any buffalo left in these parts.'

'I wouldn't expect to catch you on a bum trick like that.' He bent forward. 'All right, Dave, stop kicking it around. I know what's going on. I'm just surprised at you, that's all. You weren't going to fight Speakman. You wanted to talk it out.'

'Still do,' said Frome. The waitress arrived with the steak, french fries and onions. After she had left, Frome continued, 'That's why I'm in town. I'll see Speakman in the morning.'

Justin still looked at Frome. 'Has it started?'

'Started?'

'Trouble. You know what I mean. Has it started?'

'When I hear of any, I'll let you know.'

'Like hell you will. You're not packing a rod because it makes you look more masculine.' He hesitated. 'Speakman's in town now. Why wait until tomorrow?'

'I'm having dinner. You ask too many questions.'

'And I don't get any answers.'

'That's because you ask the wrong people.'

'Glinton and you fallen out over something?' Justin pushed at him suddenly. 'Or have you and Hesta broken off your engagement?'

44

'Now you're getting personal, Sam. Hell, making you a lawman hasn't done you any good, Sam. You're suspecting trouble under every bush.'

Justin flushed angrily. 'I'm expecting trouble, but not from under bushes. Speakman's brought a pack of gunhawks, but I don't kid myself they're here for their health or to knock over our bank. Glinton's buying guns to furnish an army.'

'So?' said Frome, slicing at his steak.

'So a warning. If this thing breaks out, there'll be no favourites. Whoever starts it, collects from me. Whether it's Speakman, you, or anybody else.'

Frome said, 'I always said you were honest, Sam. Shut the door after you, huh?'

Justin got up, glowered at the rancher a moment, then left angrily without looking back.

Curly saw that Frome was annoyed because he had quarrelled with the sheriff who was obviously a close friend. She spent the rest of the meal telling the rancher of the funny things that had happened while the touring company were on the road. Frome relaxed and forgot his troubles.

After the meal, he returned Curly to the saloon. They went in at the side entrance from the alley. Curly stopped at the door, extended her hand through her coat, and said, 'Thank you, Dave, for a very pleasant hour.'

Frome took her hand, held it a moment longer than was necessary, and countered, 'Well, if you enjoyed it, Curly, we must do it again.'

She frowned. 'Would that be wise? It's not my business, but the sheriff said you were engaged . . . you know how people talk . . . small town.'

Frome smiled. 'Not to worry. What harm is there in taking a bite to eat together?'

'We'll see,' she said. 'Meanwhile, I have to be ready for the next show.'

Frome returned to the bar at the front of the saloon. He was leaning there ten minutes later, when Matt Grape and Dwight Taber, a tall cowpuncher who had worked for Frome, but who now probably worked for the Double Star, came through the batwings. Both riders slapped alkali dust from their clothes, then moved towards Frome.

Frome ordered them a couple of beers, and nodded. Grape said, 'Kyle's plenty sore about the Talbot killing. He got back about an hour after the incident. When he found you'd gone, he took it out on me because I'd given you the gun and got you from the canyon. He tried to fire me. But Glinton put him in his place. Reminded him that the trouble's with the miners – not with you. Taber and I left shortly after. We went to the Canyon, did the necessary for Wolf, then came on here. It'll give Kyle time to cool down.'

Frome said, 'Was he shaken or just angry?'

Grape said, 'Angry. Talbot was a pal of his. Kyle's no coward. He'll face you, Dave.'

'I'm looking forward to it.'

'You might have a wait. Kyle's been ordered to lay off you. Glinton told him to concentrate on the miners.'

'So – I can wait.'

There was sarcasm in the ramrod's reply. 'Yeah, but where are you going to wait?'

Frome shrugged. 'Here's as good a place as any. I can see Speakman here. If you're expecting me to ride down miners in the hills. . . .' He scowled.

46

'And if Speakman won't listen – which he won't – what'll your cattle drink?'

'There's water in the Teap.'

'Won't be long before that's copper-contaminated.'

'So,' Frome grinned, 'I'll advertise my stuff as copper-plate steaks. And, anyway, I've been thinking of another way to get water. Drill wells. Drill down far enough, and you can have a pond in your own back yard.'

'I'll believe it when I see it.' Grape's voice softened. 'You haven't got a crew left, Dave, you know that? They've joined up with Glinton. Only Long Will's at the Broken Arrow. But any time you feel like getting tough with Speakman, the boys will come back. You know that, too, don't you?'

Frome shrugged. 'There's nothing important for a month or two. Only that army contract to fill, and that's way off. I'll soon round up a crew to drive that herd.'

Grape nodded. 'Could be that everything would've been settled by then.'

Frome unbuckled the shellbelt and held it out to Grape. 'Thanks for the loan.'

Grape hesitated. 'What about Bennett?'

'You said he won't be making any moves yet. Besides, Gulick's got Colts for sale.'

'OK.' Grape buckled on the gun. 'It's Glinton's, anyway.' He turned to Taber, finished his beer. 'Well, I guess we'll be moving. This isn't our kind of bar.'

Frome said, 'I'm heading for the hotel. I need some sleep.'

They went through the batwings, stood on the sidewalk.

Grape was embarrassed. Frome said, 'Forget it, Matt. A

47

hundred bucks says you'll be back ramrodding for me in a month.'

'I hope so.'

Frome nodded to Taber, and crossed to the hotel. Grape and the cowpuncher swung left, moving along Main.

Frome reached the hotel and found the lobby and bar to the left packed. Most of the men bore the stamp of hard case gun-slingers. He reached the reception desk and was told that the room he usually took on the first floor was occupied.

He took a small coffin-like room on the third floor, and made the long climb. He found it at the end of a dingy corridor at the rear of the hotel.

He looked at the little room, shrugged, began to undress. He was that tired, he couldn't care less.

He locked the door and went to sleep.

CHAPTER 7

Frome heard the voice and came awake. The room was still dark with night's shadows, but dawn was a dirty grey above his window. The voice came again, and he recognized it, and came up on the bed.

'Dave! Dave! Wake-up, Dave!'

It was Sam Justin, and something in his voice brought Frome awake. 'What is it, Sam?'

'Bad news. Open up.'

Frome came off the cot, crossed to the door, unlocked and opened it, a question taking shape on his lips as the sheriff lumbered in.

'Dave, this is pretty bad.' The sheriff stumbled over the words. 'Matt Grape and Dwight Taber are dead.'

It took long seconds to sink in, to believe. 'What – what are you saying, Sam?'

Justin smacked his hands together. 'They didn't have a chance. It was a massacre.'

'How did it happen?' Frome said softly. 'Where?'

Justin walked to the window. He looked out. He didn't look back as he talked. 'About two hours ago . . . just as the night spots were closing down . . . a bunch of riders, maybe

49

four or five, shot off their handguns at a corner. Nobody wondered about it ... thought they were just letting off steam ... then one of my deputy's found the bodies. Both had been hit several times ... both were dead ... and neither had had the chance tc get their guns out.'

Frome went cold. He sank on to the cot. It was something he didn't want to believe, but that didn't mean it had not happened. It was a cold fact. No amount of wishing would make it any different. 'Who did it, Sam?'

Justin shrugged. 'We don't know.'

'What do you mean – you don't know? What kind of sheriff are you, anyway. You're the man who's supposed to know everything!'

Justin turned slowly. 'OK, Dave, kick me if it'll make you feel any better.'

'Sorry.'

'That's all right. I've been working on it. Got a couple of deputies still working on it. Matt and Taber went to the Pioneer. Spent most of the time there, excepting for a break to catch some food. Spencer, who runs the Pioneer, says the boys kept to themselves. They didn't talk to anybody other than a couple of cowpokes, and they didn't quarrel with anybody. Same happened at the eatery. They didn't argue with anybody. Only cowfolk use the Pioneer' – Justin looked at Frome sharply – 'so couldn't be that they, in some way, annoyed any miners. And, as you've already told me, trouble hasn't started yet.'

'Nobody saw the horsemen?'

'Several people saw the bunch firing off their irons, but they were too far away to recognize them. They didn't think anything of it. It must've been that crowd, though, because that was the only firing heard on that street.'

Frome bunched his fist. 'We'll get the sonsofbitches, Sam. First thing you do, is post a reward. Five thousand dollars just for the names. No "dead or alive" mush. Just the names.'

'OK,' Justin said. 'I'm thinking about it, and I don't see it as an accident. Nor as a grudge shooting. Everybody liked Grape, and Taber was an easy-going guy. And even if they annoyed say a bunch of miners . . . well, the shovel-heads are pretty rough, but I doubt if they'd do something foul like this.'

Frome said, 'What are you getting at, Sam?'

'Just this. I think somebody's out to get you. Grape was close to you – very close. I think that in someway this links up with you.'

Frome didn't answer. He was thinking about the lynching of Denny Le Roy and Tony Wolf. Was the murder of his two boys the miners' reply to the Wolf killing?

Frome reflected, too, that Justin didn't know about the deaths of Denny Le Roy and Tony Wolf.

He wondered whether or not he should tell Justin. Then he decided against it. If the miners had killed Grape and Taber, then Frome couldn't afford to do any favours for Justin. The sheriff was neutral, opposing all force. If Speakman had ordered the gunning of Grape and Taber as a reprisal for Tony Wolf, then that put Frome irrevocably in a range war against the miners.

Justin was looking at him now. 'What do you think, Dave? Do you think somebody's out to get you?'

Frome said, 'Speakman – what about Speakman? You said he's got gunslingers with him.'

Justin looked scared. 'Now, Dave, hang on a moment. Don't let's do any wild guessing. Why should Speakman pull a deal like this? Especially on your men? He knows you're the only rancher who wants to find a peaceful solution.'

'I wouldn't know for sure,' Frome said. 'But I'll tell you one thing, I'm going to find out.'

'Now, Dave, you hold on. Matt was a friend of mine, too. There's a lot about this I don't understand. I think you're holding something back. You think Speakman, but why?'

Frome began to dress. 'Just a guess. Where have you taken Matt and Taber?'

'The undertakers.' Justin swung to the door. He paused there. 'Don't do anything stupid. Leave it to the law. We'll find out who those gunhawks were.'

'We'll see about that,' Frome said. 'I'm not hanging about on this thing until Grape's death is just a distant memory.'

Justin snarled. 'I told you, I'll handle it. Get in my way, go off half-cocked, and I'll slap you in jail.'

'Just try it,' Frome said.

Justin left, slamming the door.

Frome finished dressing. He crossed to the small wash-stand, poured water into the basin, and quickly washed. He left the hotel a few minutes later, stood on the boardwalk and looked down the empty street. The early morning breeze touched him. In the mud a few yards away two dogs fought over a scrap of something. A lone rider swung from an alley further down, hunched forward in the saddle of his small cowpony, slicker pulled to his hat-brim, heading for some distant range after blowing a month's wages in a few swiftly-passing hours.

Light still touched the windows of The Drovers and Frome, guessing that Mike Sturmer would still be cleaning up the bar, crossed the street and moved along to the saloon. He pushed through the batwings and saw Mike Sturmer behind the bar. He was busy counting up the night's takings.

He was surprised to see Frome. 'Hey, couldn't you sleep?'

Frome guessed that he hadn't heard about the Grape-Taber shooting. He crossed to the bar, took out his makings, laid them on the bar. 'Couldn't sleep.'

Sturmer was pushing coins into a cloth bag. Two negro cleaners had piled the chairs on to tables and were scrubbing the floor. Right at the end of the saloon, Frome saw the stage and it's glittering decorations and remembered Curly. His lips softened with the memory.

'Can I get you something?' Sturmer said.

'Not from behind the counter you can't, Mike. But I could go a cup of coffee if your kitchen's working.'

'Always is.' Sturmer told one of the cleaners to fetch two mugs of coffee. 'I don't like it myself,' he said, 'but a feller shouldn't drink alone.'

Frome fashioned a cigarette. 'Curly asleep?'

Sturmer looked up, nodded.

'A nice kid,' Frome said.

'Yeah, Curly's a nice kid, Dave.' He frowned. He looked at Frome a moment, and he said, 'Don't kick me for saying this, Dave, but . . . but she's different to the usual run of saloon girl. She's not used to men, could easily get hurt, if you savvy what I mean.'

Frome smiled. 'I savvy.'

Sturmer gave a nervous laugh. 'She's had one unhappy experience, I hear tell. I wouldn't like for her to have another. I think she's a bit struck on you, Dave. Asked questions about you. And you're engaged, get me?'

Frome lit the cigarette. 'I get you. And what do you mean by "she's had one unhappy experience?" '

'Don't know all the facts. But it appears Curly was engaged to some fellow who got killed in a gunfight.'

Frome considered that. He thought that that could happen to him. His mind went back to the deaths of Grape and Taber. He also had to see Speakman. He decided he wanted to see Speakman very badly now. The deaths of his two men, following on the lynching of Tony Wolf, must be Speakman's work.

'When does Gulick open his store, Mike?' he asked.

'At eight. Dead on eight.'

Frome smiled wryly at Sturmer's phrasing. He would buy a handgun from Gulick dead on eight, and he might very well be dead on nine.

The negro came across the long saloon with mugs of steaming coffee.

CHAPTER 8

Frome stood outside Ebb Gulick's store a few minutes before eight o'clock, his back resting against a tie-rack, big fingers expertly shaping a cigarette. Around him Main came alive, the rustle and bustle increasing in tempo as the town began a fresh day.

Ott Dakers opened the door of his barber shop opposite, saluting Frome, flexing his muscles and breathing heavily, driving sleep from his narrow frame. Ott took down his shop shutters and disappeared into his shop.

A fleet of Merivales, teams straining, turned on to Main from the railhead and rattled by, carrying goods for Denton and other small cow towns beyond the Arrows. A few riders, miners and cowpokes, swung from livery stables, grim-jawed and heavy-eyed after a night's carousing.

Suddenly a group of men swung from the hotel, spurs jangling on the boardwalk. Frome stiffened with interest when he saw George Broome, the mining district officer, among them. Then he saw the tall man beside Broome and looked him over closely. The man was well-dressed in

Eastern clothes, looked confident and was full of his own importance. It had to be Speakman, Frome thought, and looked at the other men. He identified them as gunslingers. His eyes narrowed. The man who had dropped Grape and Taber could be here.

And then Frome saw Broome nudge the tall man, and whisper. The tall man looked across at Frome, then swung towards the boardwalk to cross the street.

Frome guessed that they were heading for Ma Connick's café for breakfast, because the food was much better there than at the hotel. He also knew that they didn't need to cross the street to get there.

Frome pretended to lose interest, looking in the opposite direction as the men came on, moving heavily, the boards thumping beneath Frome. Frome looked up just before they reached him. He saw that Speakman, if indeed the man was Speakman, had pushed out ahead, a tall, toothy gunslinger at his elbow.

'Are you Frome?' the man sneered.

Frome said very softly, 'I am.'

'I'm Peter Speakman. I'm warning you here and now, Frome, that I won't tolerate any interference from you cowboys in the Arrows. That clear?'

'You couldn't make it any clearer,' Frome said.

'Well?' Speakman snapped, not liking the indifference Frome showed.

Frome said, 'We'll discuss that matter later. In private.'

Speakman moved forward, menace building in his expression. 'Don't play cat-and-mouse with me, Frome. I've heard about you. You don't frighten anybody.' He looked down at the rancher's belt, saw no gun there. 'So you run and tell your more war-like friends what I've said. Pronto.'

Frome said easily, 'You tell them – pronto.'

The gunfighter pushed forward. His lips were compressed in a tight smile. 'He's talking big on account he don't carry a gun.'

Speakman looked around warily. 'Hold on, Chet. Too many folk about.' He glared. 'You watch your tongue, cowboy.'

Frome's eyes narrowed. 'You don't frighten me, Speakman. On your way. I've got a few things I want to talk about, I'll see you in business hours.'

Speakman's lips worked. He calmed suddenly. Then he moved. 'Talk to him, Chet,' he said.

Frome turned, words piling into his throat, looking to the fast-moving Peter Speakman – and then the gunhawk struck.

His gloved fist exploded in the pit of Frome's stomach. His other fist chopped round and caught the rancher on the cheek as he jack-knifed forward. Frome collapsed off the sidewalk, rolling into the hoof-churned mud beneath the horse rack. He rolled over on his back, fighting for breath, trying to drag himself upright.

The gunfighter crouched over him. 'You've got an errand to run, sucker. Mount and ride. Pass the word. Don't do the errand, and you'll hear from me. I'm Chet Dager. You'll hear a lot about me in this territory before long.'

Frome, sucking at air, tried to drag up and reach for the gunman. Dager's hand dropped to his gun. 'Try it and I'll drill you. My breakfast's waiting. I ain't got time to wrassle with a muddy bum like you.' He laughed, the moustached mouth tight against his big teeth. 'And don't bother Mister Speakman. He's a busy man. I see you about

Plattsville again, I'll horsewhip you out.'

Frome smiled slowly, and Chet Dager saw that smile, and it puzzled him a little. He began to move away, walking quickly to catch up Speakman and the others.

Frome pulled himself towards the boardwalk, dragging at the spur-gouged woodwork, then reaching for the knotched pole of the rack. Ott Dakers hurried from his barber shop with a towel. 'They shouldn't have done that, Mister Frome, they shouldn't have.'

Frome took the towel, wiped the mud from hands and face, and rested over the rack. 'He'll regret it, Ott,' he whispered. He saw Speakman and his crowd recross the street and disappear into Ma Connick's further down Main.

Frome was wiping the mud from his shirt with a grimed towel when Ebb Gulick's son, the broom-stick thin Al, came hurrying on to Main. He put on more speed on seeing Frome. A key appeared in his hand. 'Sorry to keep you waiting, Mister Frome,' he said, as he unlocked the door.

Frome said, 'You're on time. But I wished you'd been five minutes earlier.' He followed the boy into the shop.

Al didn't understand, but he didn't puzzle over it. Al thought there was a lot of things he didn't understand, but he thought that was because of his age.

Frome following Gulick into the store. It was dark until the boy pulled the shutters. The atmosphere was stuffy, the smell was undefinable, a mixture of a thousand and one articles. Expecting the rancher to produce a list of canned goods, Al Gulick dived behind the counter. But Frome had walked the length of the store and was inspecting the Colts that swung in shellbelts on the wall. He finally selected a pair of matching, black-handled forty-fives in cutaway black leather and conch-studded holsters.

He strapped on the belt, tested the guns in clearance and weight, then began to feed shells into them. Gullick came along, looking surprised.

Frome loaded then span the cylinders, and moved to a rack of rifles. He selected a Winchester, tested the action, passed it to Gulick and told him to find a saddle boot to fit. 'I'll pick it up later, Al, and throw in a couple of boxes of shells.'

Frome was moving from the store when he saw the row of buggy whips. He lifted one, flipped it. 'I'll take this too.'

'Didn't know you had a buggy, Mister Frome.'

'I haven't.'

On the point of asking Frome if he wanted a buggy to go with the whip, Al hesitated. It wouldn't sound right. He shrugged. He couldn't understand why Frome wanted the whip. But then there was a lot of things he didn't understand.

Frome left the store. Ott Dakers, washing his windows, saw the rancher start down the street, wearing the guns and carrying a whip. Ott dived back into his shop.

Old Hank Mathers, astraddle a chair on the stage station, came up as Frome passed. He didn't know what was going on, but he hadn't lived eighty-five years by taking chances. He slipped into an alley, moving fast. It took a wise man to know when to duck out.

Just before reaching Ma Connick's plain, clapboard eatery, Frome stepped from the boardwalk and moved across the muddy street until he faced the door. He could see nobody sitting at the windows. Bending, he sent the buggy whip spinning through the door. Then he moved back, watching both door and windows, ready to drop if Dager opened fire from the cover of the door.

A minute passed before Dager showed. He poked his head from the shack, saw Frome, noted the gunbelt, then slid from the door, cat-like, his back against the wall, looking both ways, checking alleys, making sure that the rancher was alone.

'You were going to horsewhip me, Dager,' Frome called. 'I've brought the necessary.'

Dager slid forward from the boardwalk, eyes narrowed, legs astraddle.

'I've changed my mind,' he said. 'Now I'm going to cripple you for life.' His head was jutted, his elbows eased back his jacket, freeing the route to his gun. When the way was free, he moved forward, working his fingers. He stopped a dozen yards from Frome. 'Nice new guns, huh. Pity you won't get the chance to use them. OK, Frome' – his voice held boredom – 'make your play.'

Frome stood relaxed. His right hand hung beneath the holster. 'You're doing an awful lot of talking for a fighting man, Dager.'

Dager's lip tightened. Then his hand blurred for his gun. Frome saw it coming before Dager moved. He had read it in the gun-fighter's eyes. Frome's right gun came effortlessly into his hand. It came up a split second ahead of Dager's. The hammer came back, it levelled, and then Frome's thumb smashed the hammer forward.

Frome's slug, with three hundred pounds of kick, slammed at Dager's gunhand. The gun skated into the mud, the kick turned the man, then sent him folding into the mud. Mud gouged up with a smacking sound. Legs kicking, eyes glazed, Dager clawed at his shattered wrist.

Moving in on him, keeping an eye directed at Ma Connick's, Frome lifted the discarded gun and sent it spinning into an alley. 'I guess we aren't going to hear things about you after all in this territory, Dager.' His voice changed. 'Get your arm fixed, fork a bronc, and get out of here. Your fighting days are over.'

Dager fixed him with a stare, lips curled back from his big teeth. He whispered, 'Speakman'll even with you.'

'I'll be waiting.' Frome moved back. People came tumbling on to the sidewalks. Hank Mathers, who'd missed it all, appeared on the sidewalk, and began to tell anybody who would listen exactly what had happened.

Frome reached the sidewalk, stepped on to it, backing away from the café on the other side of the street. A crowd had gathered around the wounded Dager, but still nobody had appeared on the step of Ma Connick's. Frome looked on down the street to see Sam Justin's red-brick office, but apparently Justin was out, for the shot hadn't brought him along.

Mike Sturmer stood at the batwings of The Drovers. 'That was a fast draw, Dave. You surprise me. Dager was quick, but you were quicker.'

Frome said easily, 'Don't forget to tell the newspapers.'

Sturmer laughed at that. 'It's a busy morning. Action on the street, Curly crying at the window.'

'Curly see it?'

'She sure did. She saw Dager tip you into the street. Then she saw you come along with the guns. She tried to break out to stop you, but I held her in. She's up in her room.'

'Reckon I ought to go and speak to her?'

'Wouldn't do any good, then it wouldn't do any harm.

61

The damage is done. She's fallen for you, I reckon.'

'Then I'll see her.'

Sturmer gave him the directions. Frome crossed the saloon, went round the cleaners who were busy spilling fresh sawdust, and went up the stairs, along the balcony, and knuckled Curly's door. She whispered softly, and Frome entered.

The room was dark with the curtains drawn. Only thin shafts of daylight entered the room. Frome saw the girl sitting on a couch, wearing a gingham dress, busy with a needle and thread. She looked at him, her eyes serious, red-rimmed.

'Morning, Curly,' Frome said. 'I thought you'd like to come out to breakfast.'

She gave a little sob, came from the couch, and Frome went forward to meet her and took her in his arms.

Frome looked down on Main. The street was alive. Harness jingled, whips cracked, drivers bawled at their straining teams. Curly spoke from the couch, but Frome didn't turn towards her. She said softly, 'Why don't you leave here for a time, Dave? Take the train to Dodge, or Kansas City.'

Frome said, 'I can't leave now.'

'Please, Dave . . . for me. If you like, I'll come with you. Just leave . . . before it's too late.'

'If I left folk would say I was a coward.'

'Why care what folk say? You will be alive, and isn't that more important?'

Frome contrasted Curly's attitude with that of Hesta's. Curly wanted him alive, and that was all that mattered. Hesta wanted him to buckle on guns and fight, and if he was killed . . . well . . . that was life.

Frome turned and moved towards Curly. 'It's just not a matter of what folk think. Or of holding my range. I don't care overmuch about that. Yesterday I would have listened, boarded that train with you. But yesterday Matt Grape and Dwight Taber were alive. They were my men, my friends.'

Curly's eyes closed and tears began to glisten on her cheeks.

Frome bent, kissed her hair, and tiptoed away. Curly said, 'It's happened to me once, a man I loved died, I won't let it happen again!'

She was still weeping when Frome left the room.

CHAPTER 9

Frome sat in the chair, crossed his legs, began to fashion a cigarette, and looked across at Sheriff Sam Justin. The sheriff sat by the barred window which overlooked Main, a rack containing shotguns, Winchester and spare Colts just behind his head. Justin, with well practised movements, could have a shotgun off the shelf, loaded, and hit the street in twenty seconds flat.

Frome smiled. 'Thought I'd call in about the Dager incident, Sam. You going to lock me up or am I a free man?'

Justin's smile was forced. 'Now, you knew that if there was a chance I had to hold you for it, you wouldn't have breezed in. You're clean. Enough witnesses – including Old Hank, who's never seen a gun fired – said Dager went for his iron first.'

Frome licked down the paper. 'Good. I'm glad that incident's cleared up.'

Justin looked at Frome speculatively. Frome was surprised. Justin said, 'Just wondering if I'm looking at a man who'll be a corpse any time now. You're a fool, Dave.

You should've drilled Dager dead centre in the head, not the hand.'

'His fighting days are over.'

'Are they? You only need one good hand to sneak up behind a fellow and give him all six shells in the back.'

'I've told Dager to leave town.'

'He's left all right. But he can sneak back. He's one of Speakman's boys.'

Frome said, 'I know. Makes you think. Narrows it down to nothing. My money says Speakman had Matt and Dwight Taber killed.'

Justin said, 'Now you're jumping to conclusions. I've been doing some figuring, Dave. I can't see any profit in it for Speakman. Look at it this way. The townsfolk like the miners, they spend a lot of money here. Speakman needs the support of the town in any moves against you ranchers. Right, looking at it in that light, can you figure a shrewd man like Speakman engineering a double murder which could set the town against him?'

'Sure,' Frome answered promptly, 'if he thought he could get away with it.'

'But what's the motive?' Justin demanded. 'The deaths of Grape and Taber don't change the situation. If anything, it makes it harder for Speakman; the ranchers suspecting him, will be more determined to fight.'

'Or,' Frome said, 'the weaker ones, suspecting Speakman, will back down, sell up, flee.'

Justin didn't answer that. Frome lit his cigarette, swung off the chair. Justin looked at him pointedly. 'Where are you heading now?'

'To see Speakman.'

Justin scowled. 'You take it easy, huh?'

Frome smiled. He loosened both Colts in their holsters, moved to the door. 'Don't forget, Sam, I'm still paying five thousand dollars reward for the names of the gunslicks who murdered Matt and Taber.'

Justin said, 'I didn't forget. I've passed the word where it'll do the most good.'

Frome closed the door and turned along the boardwalk. He stopped at the mining office, hand on the doorknob. He looked through the glass into the dark interior. There was only an elderly clerk curled over a giant ledger in the main office. The door to George Broome's office stood open, his chair vacant, the room silent. Frome shrugged, moved away. Speakman wasn't in, but there was no hurry, he had all day.

He moved along the boardwalk, entered Ma Connick's and ordered eggs, ham, flapjacks and coffee. He ate in silence, sitting in a corner, eyes on the door. He finished the meal, paid for it, then called in at Gulick's store and collected and signed a receipt for the Winchester and the saddleboot Gulick had found for it.

He came out of the store, stood on the boardwalk. There were more than a score of friends he could call on, but Frome didn't fancy talking, not now, not after the gunfight. He wanted to talk to Speakman, and only the mine boss. Well, he could wait, and he could keep off the street and catch up on some sleep.

Moving quickly, he returned to the Plattsville Hotel.

Karno, the manager, nodded to Frome as he crossed the lobby. The man looked as if he would welcome a conversation with Frome, who had always been one of his best patrons. Frome, guessing that Karno would want to apologise because he could not offer him a good room, did not stop. He climbed the stairs to the third floor, moved along the passage, and arrived at the room. He saw a door fitted into the wall at the end of the corridor, only a yard away. He moved to it, found it unlocked, and opened it. Wooden steps led down to the yard. Frome scratched at his jaw.

He closed it, wishing a key was in the lock, then entered his own small room. He locked the door, put the bucketed repeater beneath the bed, then laid down on the cot, removing his gunbelt and draping it over the bed iron.

Within minutes he was asleep.

Frome opened his eyes. Bright sunlight slanted down across his chest from the high window. The first thing he saw was the grimed ceiling, then the battered furniture. It took him a moment to remember where he was, and then he came wide awake, swinging up off the cot, sweat beading him, knowing that something had woken him. He probed his memory – something like a board creaking?

He slid off the bed, lifted a Colt from a holster, and moved to the door on stockinged feet. He noticed the indenture at the left of the door between the chest of drawers, and he squeezed in there, his head against the door jamb, listening.

No nearby sounds reached him. The only noises were far off, on Main, harness-jingle, piano-music, saloon-laughter. A minute passed. Frome relaxed. He guessed he had been wrong, that overstrung nerves had spooked him. But he waited a moment longer. And then there came more movement, a board creaked clearly, as if a heavily-built man had shifted weight. Frome bent forward, knowing that the room was too small, that he was a sitting duck. His hand reached for the key, to turn it, to bounce out into the hall. But he was too late. Whoever was outside the door had now decided that a silent approach was no longer necessary.

The door to the yard bounced open suddenly. Heavy footsteps sounded. They stopped at Frome's door. Gun hammers clicked back. A harsh voice whispered, 'Make it quick!'

Frome realized he was trapped. He slid tightly into the wall. Then the guns began to kick. Slugs gouged through the door's thin wood, leaving white grooves in the dark paintwork. Bullets kicked off the cot springs, making musical sounds. Metal slashed the walls, bringing down plaster, wallpaper and brickdust. The men fanned triggers on six-shooters, turning their guns this way and that to pepper the room. The china basin on the wash-stand disintegrated with a bell-like sound.

A momentary pause. Empty guns were holstered, new guns came up. Conceding that Frome might have had time to duck beneath the cot or into a corner, the assassins lowered their aim, firing downwards. Bullets slashed the linoleum to ribbons, whipped up a small carpet and balled it, bounced off the iron bed stands with a banshee sound.

'Corners!' came a shout above the roar and echo of gunshots. The guns barked again, turned at an angle. A slug missed Frome by inches, ploughing a neat white ridge across the chest of drawers. The mirror shattered into a thousand diamonds.

Then the guns stopped, but it took Frome a moment to realize it. The echo of the shots was still there, he was almost deafened. Then he heard fast-retreating footsteps as boots hit hollow boards. Frome jack-knifed forward, turning the key in the smashed door.

As he dragged it open, he heard the door to the yard skid back. Then he was in the hall, pushing through the haze of cordite and brickdust. It caught at his throat, smartened his eyes. He saw the door to the yard still quivering. It had been slammed and hadn't closed properly. He reached it, dragged it open. Sunlight hit him. He dropped to the floor, poking head and gunhand through the door.

Feet thumped the wooden steps just below and to the right of him. He could not see the running men because his head was flat with the platform, but he didn't have to see them. He poked his gun over, judging the level, and triggered off two shots. Then he came up, hearing a scream, and then two bullets gouged through wood inches from him, and the door bounced and shuddered on its hinges.

Frome took a chance, straightened, looked forward into the yard. Two horsemen sat saddle there, holding the reins of two more mounts, and had carbines trained on the door to hold off pursuit. Looking down the steps as he turned and dropped to the platform again, Frome saw the two assassins reach the bottom of the steps. He flashed his gun up, fired once, then flopped down as the horsemen, on their spooky mounts, pumped shots up at him. The carbine shots came at the door and brickwork in a precisioned stream, holding Frome to cover. Inching forward to the rim almost, Frome poked his Colt forward and triggered off the remaining shots in the direction of the horsemen.

He sagged back then, moving back to the safety of the door, dropping his empty Colt, looking back down the hallway, thinking of his other Colt, and more importantly, of the Winchester carbine beneath the bed. But there wouldn't be time. Already he could hear the harsh rasp of voices and the slam of hoofs as the men bounced into saddles and turned the nervous mounts for the gate of the yard.

The shooting had stopped. Frome came up on the balls of his feet in a lurch, determined to see the men and try and tab their faces and dress. It had come to him that these must be the men who had killed Matt Grape and Dwight Taber.

He saw three horsemen, low along their saddles, thunder out of the gate. And then he saw the fourth man, flat on his face in the dust, and the man's spooked mount, moving stiff-leggedly around the yard. Frome didn't hesitate. He scooped up his empty Colt and hurried down the steps in his stockinged feet. He watched the man, and the horse, seeing the seven-shot Spencer carbine in its saddlebucket. He hoped the long gun was loaded.

As he jumped over the dropped man, he saw the pool of blood seeping across the man's back. His bullet had hit the man in the back, driving through into his heart. Frome thought grimly that the man would drive no more slugs through hotel doors.

The hard ground tore at his stockinged feet as Frome crossed the yard, cornering the jumpy bronc. He reached it, jerked the carbine from the bucket, and swung up into the saddle, dragging the horse round with a brutal tug on the reins. He heeled the bronc towards the gate, jacking a bullet into the firing position of the carbine with a slick-slack sound.

Hoofbeats sounded from beyond the sagging wooden fence, pointing the way for Frome. The riders had gone left, turning down the rash of alleys, heading for open country. Frome hit the gate, dragging the pony left, forward in the saddle, urging the pony with his heels.

He saw the three men strung out in a line ahead, twenty yards away, pushing their broncs down the narrow, curving alley at maddening and dangerous speeds. Using the Spencer with one hand, Frome fired at the last of the men. The butt slammed him under the armpit in recoil, he saw the rider skid sideways in his saddle, but he managed to keep his perch. Frome cursed, jacked in a fresh shell, holding the carbine under his arm, then aimed again. He waited until the pony ahead had taken a shallow dip and was coming up. Then he fired, driving the shell between the man's shoulder blades. The impact of the heavy shell smacked the man over the head of his racing pony. The spooking, rearing bronc stopped dead, skidding, then jammed its head in close to the wall, blocking the alley. The rider didn't stir on the alley's floor. He lay spreadeagled, still clutching the reins.

Frome fired twice more down the alley at the other men, but missed. Then the two riders had swung from sight. Frome brought his bronc to a stop to pass the dead man's skittish animal. He prodded the animal with the carbine as he passed to clear the way.

He took a quick look at the fallen man as he put the pony to a gallop. His lips hardened with recognition. The dead man was Clint Farrow, who he had fired from the Broken Arrow for carrying a gun.

He kicked the pony forward.

CHAPTER 10

Frome came out of the alley and turned the pony on to open ground. A hundred and fifty yards ahead he saw the two survivors. Low along their mounts, they were swinging for a brush-covered escarpment. Frome pushed forward.

The two riders reached the embankment, lashing their mounts up the steep sides. The mounts began to climb, twisting and skidding, sending up a dust cloud. They reached the ridge top when Frome was still halfway across, and disappeared, smashing through timber.

Frome took more care, pinpointing an easier climb, swerving the bronc towards it. He reached it, high and forward in the saddle, helping the pony to make the climb. The two men were riding their mounts into the ground, it seemed to Frome. Eventually, if he held his pony in check, he must overtake them.

With a lunge, which sent shale spilling, the pony reached the rim, went over the hump, and entered the timber. Branches snapped back before rider and mount. They burst into the open, coming on to a shelf of meadow, and Frome saw the men two hundred yards ahead of him, driving lathered foamed ponies toward the dried-up bed of the Muleshoe River.

Frome kneed the pony, veering to the right, away from the men, to where the ground sloped down. Moments later through sweat-drenched eyelids, he saw the riders disappear over the river's lip, a dust pall climbing above the spot as the mounts skidded down the sides. Frome smiled, and still drove his pony right of the point. The meadow ended suddenly. Hard ground fell away beneath the cracking hoofs of the pony.

Frome knew he was taking a gamble, but he considered the odds were on his side. He still veered right. The men, he had figured, would turn right in the river bed, driving for open country. If they turned left, it would take them in close to the railhead at Plattsville, and the men wanted to get away from people.

The ground beneath the racing pony changed again. Now it was sand-patchy, rock-strewn. No dust betrayed the movement of the men from above the river bed.

Frome kept right, aiming for a point of the bank higher up. He was still yards from the rim, when he sprang impatiently from the saddle. The rough ground tore at his stockinged feet as he headed for the rim, hefting the carbine.

Reaching the edge, he dropped, cuffing the sweat from his face to clear his eyes. He looked over the rim to the dry bed, twenty-five feet beneath him. The bed twisted and curved sharply, and he found his view was obstructed by a rock outcropping which jutted out a hundred feet to his left.

He poked the rifle over the rim, jacked in a shell, and waited. Far off along the bed, he heard the drum of hoofbeats. The sound increased. The horses seemed to be coming fast, and this surprised him, for he imagined that the ponies driven by the men were on the point of dropping by now.

The horses came on fast, too fast to please Frome. Then the sound came from just beyond the outcropping and Frome realized that more than two horses were coming. His lips tightened. There had been other gunhawks waiting in the bed for the four men, and he only had three shells left! Frome aimed for a sandy patch just beyond the cropping, determined to make his three shots show a hundred per cent profit.

And then three riders burst into view. All were mounted on fresh-looking, fast-moving cowponies, and Frome knew the answer: they had left a man in the river bed with get-away mounts.

Frome sighted on one man, pressed the trigger, lifted the carbine, jerking in a fresh shell. The bullet drove down into the man, side-swiping him from his saddle. Frome aimed on the next man, fired, but the man had already moved to jack back and turn his dancing mount. Sand tulipped just beyond the man. Frome cursed; jacked in the last shell.

The two riders had swerved. One horse sank down, losing its grip on the sandy floor, rightened, turned the outcropping. Frome came up, aiming at the last man in view as he swung his horse, lashing it fiercely towards cover. Frome fired just before the man disappeared, and saw his buckskin jacket flair up as his arm snaked out. Frome smiled as the man disappeared; at least he had winged the man.

More hoofbeats sounded, coming towards him around the outcropping. Surely, Frome thought, the men were not going to try and ride by him? They wouldn't know that his carbine was empty. And then three horses came round the outcropping, saddled but riderless, spooked and confused, and Frome realized that two of these at least had been for Farrow and the man who died in the yard.

A shot cracked out, smoke billowing from a point of the outcropping. Frome saw one of the ponies go down, and realized that the shot had not been aimed at him. Another shot followed a split second later and another riderless horse turned a somersault. The third shot took the last pony, and it skidded down on its legs. With an empty carbine, flinty-eyed and tight-lipped, Frome had to watch the ponies die. He knew the two killers were shooting down the fresh mounts so that Frome couldn't give them further chase.

And then Frome saw a strange sight. The man who he had dropped came up, his righthand clawing at a shattered shoulder, and staggered towards the out-cropping; four shots smacked the man to the ground. Frome smiled harshly. The two men, not sure that their companion could travel far and fast, were making sure that he wouldn't remain behind to talk to the sheriff.

A moment later there came the tattoo of hoofs. The two riders were retreating along the Muleshoe's bed. Hefting the empty Spencer, Frome began to work down the bank to the bed, carefully picking the soft spots because of the pain from his feet.

When he reached the bottom the hoofbeats were only a whisper in the distance. He hurried across to the dead man, scooping up the handgun from his holster. Frome's bullet had taken the man high in the shoulder, shattering bone, but the shots of his companions had driven into his heart and stomach. Frome then moved to one of the dropped ponies, dragged a Winchester from the bucket. It was then that he saw the brand on the pony's rump. He cursed softly, moved closer to inspect it, then checked the brand on the other two ponies. He swore again, this time loudly. The men had not only tried to kill him, they had stolen his own branded Broken Arrow cowponies to use in the getaway.

Frome wondered what brand he would find on the pony he had ridden from the yard. Checking that the Winchester was loaded, he climbed back to the top of the river bank, and moved to the pony which was ground anchored by the reins.

Turning the pony he saw that it carried the O Diamond brand. He frowned. The O Diamond was the registered brand of Old Jacob Haines who owned a blooded horse outfit near Denton on the other side of the Arrows.

Frome mounted the pony and started it along the river bank. He had only covered a few yards when he saw dust climb in a thick cloud a half a mile along the river. The two men had not gone on to the railhead, but were forking off. Watching from the halted pony, he saw the men appear momentarily on the rim, then swing down, disappearing in open country.

Still thinking about the O Diamond and Broken Arrow brands on the ponies, Frome swung for Plattsville.

CHAPTER 11

Frome was on his third mug of coffee when Sam Justin
came back to his office. He saw that the sheriff was hefting
a burlap sack, and that the man was in a bad temper.
'That's right, Dave, make yourself at home. Use the office,
but don't use the law officers.'

Frome looked up from the smoke he was rolling. 'Don't
understand you, Sam?'

Justin put the bag on his desk. 'It's quite simple.
Plenty's been happening out in the cow country which I
ought to know about. You haven't told me a thing. I sent
one of my deputies – Sloane – out to the Double Star.
Glinton gave the cold treatment. Also, he found that he'd
entered an armed camp. Nobody would talk to him, even
old friends buttoned their lips. You don't seem to be
wanted there, but most of your crew seem to be on
Glinton's payroll. There's also other men riding in, real
hard cases.'

Frome shrugged. 'To get back to the point, what about
this attempt on my life at the hotel?'

Justin glowered, tipped the bag up. A half a dozen Colts
rattled on to the desk. There were two watches, several

Bull Durham sacks, matches and other odds and ends. Justin reached into his pocket, brought out a handful of bank notes and coins and slapped them on his desk beside the guns. 'That's all of it, no wallets, no names. The only one we know is Farrow who used to work for you. Karno, the hotel manager, recognized the dead man in the yard as a hombre who'd been sitting in the hotel all morning, probably looking for you.'

'That fits.'

'I went out to the Muleshoe, found those spent ponies the killers had used to get away from the hotel. Like the one you rode, they're O Diamond stock. I also found that the men, all five of them, had been camped in the bed for at least a day. There were two burned-out campfires, some groceries, and food waste.'

'It looks as if they're the boys who got Matt and Dwight Taber.'

Justin agreed to that.

'What surprises me,' Frome said, 'is that Farrow would take miners' money – even if he wanted to get even with me.'

Justin's face tightened with anger. 'There you go again, jumping to conclusions. There's not a shred of evidence that Speakman was behind it.'

Frome got up. 'Look, the play was well organized. There were five men, all top guns with changes of horses. It looked well-planned, and costly. Farrow wanted to get even with me, but where would the kid get the dough to hire on four top guns?'

'I'm not suggesting Farrow was behind the deal. He was only a part of it. What I'm saying is you can't say it was Speakman until you're sure. Speakman brought some fifteen gunmen with him. They booked in at the hotel. I've checked their movements for last night. When Matt and Taber were killed, most of these guns were gambling in two saloons on Main. The rest were eating at Ma Connick's with Pete Speakman.'

'All right. There's another way to look at it. Speakman left these men out at the Muleshoe, kept them back and hidden just in case he needed them for a raw killing job. He made no obvious contact with them. They were brought in to do one job, and only one job, and then to head out.'

Justin considered that a moment. 'Could be, but we still don't have the proof.'

'You can make it finer than that, Sam,' Frome said. 'It looks as if these boys were hurried in to do a quick job and didn't intend to stay too long.'

'How can you be so specific?' Justin snapped.

Frome said. 'The stolen horses. They lifted O Diamond stock and my Broken Arrow ponies. They wanted a relay of mounts for a fast get away. Had they been intending to stay, would they have moved about with stolen stock? Anybody could have spotted them in the Muleshoe. Anybody seeing strangers camped in the Muleshoe with Broken Arrow broncs and O Diamond would've reported the matter to you.'

'That makes sense,' Justin conceded. 'Unless these gunnies had a specific job to do, they wouldn't know how long they were here for. And if they didn't know that, they'd be awful careful in "borrowing" horses.'

'I'd say,' Frome said thoughtfully, 'that the men didn't figure they'd be near Plattsville for more than a day and a night.'

'You know that Speakman's left,' Justin said, suddenly changing the subject. 'Left with all his gunnies about an hour ago – just before the shooting up at the hotel. Rode out along the Plattsville Road heading for the mines.'

Frome scowled. 'I'll see him when he gets back.'

Justin said, 'That's your business. I'd hate to lose a friend, even if he no longer confides in me, so don't try and take that crowd on all at once.'

Frome grinned. 'I'll watch it.' He got up. 'I won't invite you to lunch with me. You'll ask too many questions, and it'll keep you from your work. Besides, I'm taking Curly to lunch.'

Justin watched him cross to the door. 'Is that wise? You're engaged to Hesta. You know how people talk?'

Frome shrugged his shoulders as if the fact that people talked didn't worry him.

'By the way,' Justin said, 'I talked to George Broome.'

Frome stopped, hand reaching for the door. 'So?'

'He doesn't like Speakman. Hates his methods, and thinks that both miners and cattlemen can get on together if they compromise. He thinks like you, is a moderate, doesn't believe in violence.'

'So?' Frome said impatiently.

'So he doesn't think Speakman was behind either the Grape-Taber murders or the attempt to nail you. He's even been down to the undertaker's and looked at the men you dropped. He doesn't remember ever seeing them with Speakman.'

'You're not telling me anything,' Frome said impatiently.

Justin lifted his finger. 'Broome made this point. That Speakman wouldn't pull off a deal like that because it

80

wouldn't get him anywhere and might annoy the townsfolk. Broome said Speakman wants the town to back him against the cattlemen. Broome agrees that Speakman's ruthless and will kill without compunction, but he says that if Speakman wanted to frighten the cattlemen, he'd burn a few ranches and kill stock – but well away from Plattsville.'

Frome said, 'It's a free country, Broome can think what he likes.'

Justin snapped, 'If I was you, I'd do a bit more thinking. I'd forget Speakman for a moment, and try and think of some other powerful party who might like to see you dead.'

Frome looked at the sheriff, saw the seriousness in the man's expression. He began to close the door behind him. 'I'll think about it,' he said.

Frome worked along the boardwalk through the crowd, crossed the street and pushed through the batwings of The Drovers. He crossed to the bar. As Mike came along, he said, 'Curly?'

Sturmer said: 'She gave up waiting. Thought you weren't coming. I heard about the shooting up at the hotel, but I've kept it from Curly. She went next door about twenty minutes ago.'

Frome saluted and left the bar. He moved along to the café and saw Curly sitting at the table by the window. She saw him, smiled, and Frome moved to the door.

He crossed the step, stopped and stiffened. Kyle Bennett and Hesta Le Roy were sitting at the next table to Curly across the gangway and overlooking the street. Frome hesitated for only a moment, wondering whether to call Curly out and go elsewhere. But it was too late;

Curly was halfway through her meal; and Hesta had seen him.

Frome turned his head away, entered the café, and slid behind the table facing Curly. The girl was smiling, her hand came forward, covering his. 'What happened, did you oversleep?'

Frome smiled, tight-lipped, and nodded. From the corner of his eyes, he saw that Bennett had put down his knife and fork and had twisted in his chair.

Bennett had his guns buckled on, but Frome knew the showdown couldn't come at this moment – not with Hesta and Curly present.

Then Bennett was talking – talking loudly – complaining.

Bennett thumped the table, gesticulating to the waitress. She came hurrying up. Curly looked around in surprise, wondered what was the matter with the man.

The waitress said, 'Is there something wrong, sir?'

'Plenty!' Bennett snapped. He indicated Hesta. 'When I bring a lady to lunch here, I don't expect that she should lunch in the presence of saloon harpies.'

The waitress began to stutter. Impatiently, Bennett swung, pointing at Curly. 'There. It's disgraceful.'

Curly whitened, moved back. Frome thought, 'That does it,' and launched himself. Bennett didn't get the opportunity to say more. Frome cleared his own table and the gangway, reached Bennett and dragged him to his feet, and swung his left fist at Bennett's jaw. Bennett smacked back through the plate glass window, and finished up on the boardwalk in a shower of cascading glass.

Frome went down the step. He met Bennett as the man

82

was coming up. Blood streaked Bennett's face. He cursed at Frome and came forward, his right whipping through Frome's defences and exploding on the rancher's cheek.

Frome skidded back, hit the door jamb. Then he darted at Bennett, ducked beneath the man's stabbing fists and guard, and belted him twice on the chest. Bennett staggered back under the weight, hit the tie-rack, and ponies began to jerk at the poles.

Bennett threw two punches. Frome stopped one, but the other came through, hitting Frome over the heart. It started old bruises there. Frome's head jerked back as Bennett caught him on the point of the chin. Pain speared down his spine. Then he was moving in on Bennett again, using his head as a ram, determined to do all the damage he could and hang the consequences to himself. Bennett's fists stabbed at his forehead and nose. Then Frome was in, cannoning against Bennett, turning the man slightly, carrying him to the wall with the weight of his charge, slamming him against it, then working both fists on Bennett's chest and face.

Then Bennett used his feet. Frome saw the kick coming, but he couldn't get out of the way in time. His leg seemed to burst into flames as Bennett's boot struck his knee. He felt the leg buckle beneath him, felt himself falling. The sidewalk came up, slamming the knee. Then Bennett was above him, a blood-stained, sweat-soaked face snarled at him. Frome saw the big punch coming. Bennett was putting everything he had into the throw. Frome swung hard to one side. The punch zipped past his head, dying, but Bennett was bringing over another 'undertaker's comforter', swinging his body behind the fist.

Frome collapsed his other leg, falling to the boards, and the punch broke air above him. Then, forcing power into his injured leg, he came up, just as Bennett was trying to retrieve his balance after loosening the punch. Frome had all the time he needed. The punch he brought up from the boards had been born down there. It crumbled Bennett's faulty defences, scraped along his shoulder, and caught his skull. Pain peeled back along Frome's arm, momentarily numbing it. Bennett grunted and skidded back against the wall. Frome went after him, his other fist working.

Bennett's hand lashed out blindly, fingers extended claw-like, probing for Frome's eyes. His fingers tightened around Frome's hair, jerking him forward. Frome went in and then he hit Bennett in the stomach. Bennett collapsed against the wall, shaking the building. Frome had all the time he needed. He stood off a yard, brought his fist over, and slammed it for Bennett's chin.

The wall rocked as Bennett bounced against it. Frome's other fist came in, catching Bennett as he was folding, sideswiping him away. Bennett hit the boardwalk heavily, face down, hands extended, his face bloodied.

Frome staggered to the hitchrack, folded against it for a minute, breathing heavily. The fight had attracted a crowd and Frome looked up into a sea of dancing faces.

Frome saw Hesta's buckboard just beyond the rack. He ordered a couple of watchers to help him. They lifted the unconscious Bennett and put him over the tailgate of the buckboard. Before turning away, Frome scooped up Bennett's hat and threw it after him.

CHAPTER 12

Frome went back into the café. Somebody brushed by him, leaving. He saw Curly standing by the table, her hand to her mouth. He took her arm, leading her deeper into the café, found an empty table and sagged heavily into the chair.

Curly sat opposite him. She was frowning. She produced a handkerchief, pushed it towards him. 'There's a cut on your forehead.'

Frome took it, put it to the cut. A hammer seemed to be clanging in his head; he had difficulty in seeing straight. In a moment he laughed. 'That was some fight. What do you think, Curly. Wasn't it a beaut?'

'Never mind what I think,' Curly said sharply. 'You should have ignored it. I'm used to such treatment.'

Frome said, 'Well, you'd better get used to not accepting such treatment.'

'That was Hesta Le Roy, wasn't it? The girl you're engaged to?'

Frome found suddenly that he didn't care. 'Was engaged to. I didn't notice any ring on her finger.'

'But then you weren't looking at her, were you?'

Frome smiled at the seriousness which showed on the girl's face. 'Did you notice the ring?'

'No.'

'But you looked, didn't you?' Frome smiled savagely. 'You looked because something told you she might be the girl. So you looked to see if she wore an engagement ring.' He bent forward, smiling. 'Tell me, Curly, was she wearing a ring?'

'She wore gloves, I . . . I couldn't see.'

'To eat food – she wore gloves to eat food?' Frome smiled.

The waitress came up. She looked firm. Her hand went to her waist, she looked at Frome pointedly, and said, 'What about the damage, Mister Frome?'

Frome said, 'Put it on the bill. Better still, go over and see my lawyer.'

'Very good, Mister Frome.' The waitress went away.

Curly got up. 'I'd better get back, Dave. My next show.'

Frome got up. 'Sorry I spoiled your lunch.' He took the handkerchief away from his forehead.' How do I look?'

She smiled then. 'You'll pass.'

Suddenly she was very beautiful and the words caught in Frome's throat. She looked at him intensely for a moment, then she turned away. He followed her from the café. Kyle Bennett had gone; and so had Hesta. They turned into the alley leading to the side entrance of The Drovers. They stopped at the door, and Curly swung suddenly and looked up at him; and he placed his arms around Curly's waist, sliding them beneath the cloak and lifting her towards him. They kissed and her arms went round his neck.

Frome whispered, 'I spoiled your lunch, so how about dinner tonight?'

'We'll see,' Curly began to break away – and then Frome heard footsteps approaching quickly. His hand sank for his gun. Mike Sturmer turned the corner. 'Dave,' he panted, 'been looking all over for you.'

'What is it?'

'Your old cook, Long Will, just rode in. Three-four minutes ago. I've got him in my office. He says somebody's rustled a whole herd of your cattle.'

Frome found it hard to believe. 'A herd?'

Sturmer swung at the door. 'Come this way . . . I'll take you to him. . . .' Frome followed Sturmer along the corridor. Curly followed him. 'He's had a hard ride . . . looks tuckered out . . . I've given him brandy.'

They swung into Sturmer's office on the right of the corridor. The old cook came up on the settee as Frome entered. He was excited, 'Dave, rustlers hit that herd of steers on the North Fork. The herd you were fattenin' for that army contract.'

Frome stopped before the cook. 'You mean they've shifted all five hundred head of them?'

'Every goddam one of them. How's that for sauce, huh?' Long Will said soberly. 'Heard shots in the distance at first light. Came from the North Fork. Since you've got nobody left to look into things, I saddled up and headed that way. Found every critter gone.'

Frome still found it hard to believe. He could understand somebody driving off a few head, but five hundred! He said, 'Are you sure it was a rustle? If some shots had been fired that way, the herd might've stampeded.'

The old cook was firm. 'I can read signs. The herd moved off in a tight bunch. Vee formation, travelling fast, but travelling tightly bunched. Crossed the Teap tightly too. They were prodded by a crew, I tell you.'

Frome said, 'Hell, who thought anybody'd have the nerve to drive off a whole herd of frisky prime beeves.'

Long Will straightened. 'Don't need a lot of nerve, Dave. There's no crew left on the place. You weren't there. Isn't much an old windbag like me can do to hold the place together.'

Frome said, 'What did you do?'

'I checked the sign to make sure. I followed all the way until the cattle crossed the Teap. Then, satisfied it was a rustle, I lit out for here fast, only stopping at the remuda herds to switch broncs on the way.'

'The herd were moved across the Teap – which way from there?'

'Swung right. Towards the Arrows. I'd guess they would be pushed through one of the passes and come out near Denton someway. Unless, of course, them rustlers turn back somewhere sharply, just to fool us.'

'But they didn't know there was anybody on the ranch, did they, so they won't need to try any tricks?' Frome countered.

'That's a fact,' Long Will said. 'Else they wouldn't have used gunfire to roll the herd. Nor hit them at daylight. If the wind hadn't been in the right direction, I doubt if I would've heard the gunfire, any how.'

Frome nodded. He was thinking. 'If I start right now, I should reach Denton late tonight or in the early hours of tomorrow.'

'You'll need to ride a couple of broncs to death to do it,' Long Will said. 'You'd better get Sam Justin and a posse.'

Frome said: 'The posse would move too slow. Not many people know the Arrows like I do. If I go alone, I stand more chance of finding fresh mounts en route. I can worry about a posse when I reach Denton. Marshal Keester can form one from there.'

Long Will moved. 'That's a good idea. Let's get moving.'

Frome said, 'You've done enough riding. You stay here.'

The old cook went to protest, but Frome was already heading for the door. Mike Sturmer and Curly followed him. Sturmer said, 'Do you think it's wise to do this alone?'

'As soon as I reach Denton, I'll get help,' Frome countered. 'I won't find trouble. The rustlers figure that they've got nothing to worry about.'

Frome was thinking that the rustlers had decided he was dead. He had now linked the rustle with the attempt on his life. The herd were moving towards Denton, and the men who had tried to kill him – and had possibly killed Grape and Taber – had used O Diamond horses. It looked as if they came in from Denton way to get him and the faithful Matt Grape, and drive off his herd, knowing that the rest of his crew had joined Glinton Le Roy's outfit and that there was nobody to stop them. Then Justin had been right. It wasn't Speakman! Justin had told him to look for some other powerful party who wanted him dead. Speakman was a mining man. He wouldn't be interested in five hundred head of cattle, nor particularly in the fifteen thousand dollars they would bring.

With Matt Grape and himself dead and out of the way, the rustlers could move off the prime beef without anybody to stop them. They could be out of the state and possibly return for further stock before the losses were noted. It would be months before Hesta Le Roy, to whom Frome had left his property in his will, would discover that the herds had been bled.

But who was behind it? Obviously a cattleman. Obviously, too, somebody who knew Frome and his ranch well. Farrow had been in it, but Farrow didn't have the brains to organize a steal like this. Who then?

Frome interrupted his thoughts, noticing that Curly had followed him. He smiled absently, 'Sorry I'll have to postpone that date for dinner.'

She was suddenly shy. 'Would you like me to ride with you, Dave?'

He chuckled. 'Not on this trip, Curly.'

She blushed angrily, 'I can ride, and I can shoot.'

He laughed, bent and kissed her, and then stepped into the alley, crossed the street, and entered the livery. He ignored the Broken Arrow bronc he'd used to ride into town. Instead, he selected a powerful corn-fed pony, hired it from the stable, saddled and rode to the hotel. Karno had his Winchester behind his counter. The manager looked miserable. Frome smiled, 'Sorry about the door, Karno, but it wasn't my slugs which did it.'

Karno held his smile in place until Frome had gone. Minutes later he had left the last house behind him, crossed the winding dried out Muleshoe River, and pushed the pony into a mile-eating lope across undulating, never-changing grasslands.

His mind returned to the problem of whom, beside Speakman, could possibly want him dead and whom would be interested and know enough to steal his cattle. He eliminated the small ranchers one by one in his mind. And then he smiled savagely as he settled on Kyle Bennett's name. He played around with the idea, fitting it into the pattern of the incidents, pushing pieces together. And he was surprised and finally horrified by what he arrived at.

It was more than just murder and a cattle rustle. Much more.

Now he recalled that it was Bennett who'd first seen the

body on the Lone Pine. He recalled also that Bennett's entire attitude preceding the finding of Denny had been keyed to expect trouble. Bennett knew trouble was coming for the very reason that he'd started it. Frome realized as the thought passed through his mind that he had no evidence to support this suspicion. But when he looked into the matter further, he saw that Kyle Bennett would be one of the first to benefit by Denny Le Roy's death – and Frome's.

Denny Le Roy was Glinton's only son who would have inherited the ranch one day. With Denny dead, Hesta inherited. Whoever married Hesta therefore would virtually own the Double Star. Hitherto, Kyle Bennett had been out of the running for Hesta's hand, but with Frome dead, he would be a strong favourite. Moreover, since he had no other kin, Frome had left a will leaving all his belongings and property to his fiancee Hesta Le Roy in the event of his death. With Denny Le Roy out of the way, and then Frome, Kyle Bennett stood a better than favourite's chance of taking over the vast grasslands and nearly thirty thousand head of cattle which comprised the double spreads.

The scope and simplicity of the plan astonished Frome. He wondered if he was just imagining it, he sought for evidence in the happenings of the last day or two to support the theory. There was little to find. There was the fact that the gunman, Martin Talbot, had been anxious to kill him before either Glinton or Hesta could interfere. But that was hardly evidence enough. There was also the fact that the assassins and the rustlers seemed to know not only Frome's movements but the grazing section of the five hundred head of prime beef. Again not evidence enough, for although Kyle Bennett would know that,

Farrow also knew it, and Farrow had been killed while riding with the men.

Frome pushed the matter at the back of his mind and concentrated on his journey. The miles had fallen behind, the corn-fed horse was fading, snorting hard, flaking off foam and saliva. Now the Double Star brand appeared on longhorns which grazed on the ocean of grass.

A tree-fringed hill swung up ahead. Frome pushed the spent pony up the climb, urging the reluctant animal forward with a rake of the spurs. The pony topped the slope, blowing hard, and pushed through a stand of wind-whipped timber. The finding of a fresh horse before the animal dropped was now a problem in Frome's mind. He knew that he should have come across groups of Glinton's half-wild remuda broncs by now. But he reflected that many of them would have been rounded up to furnish Le Roy's swollen crew with spare mounts.

A meadow rose sharply on his left and touched something in his memory. He swung the horse that way, remembered the sheltered valley beyond it and the stream. Ponies favoured Creek Valley.

He put the horse up the rim, broke through a stand of pine, and saw a dozen half wild mustangs in the water. He slackened off pace sharply, not wanting to spook them, and moved down the slope, loosening his rope. The mustangs swung at his approach, watched him a moment, then, noting his casual approach, continued feeding and drinking. He looked them over, decided they were a poor bunch, but spotted two passable ponies among them.

One, a small, barrel-chested paint, had recently been ridden, judging by the saddle marks, the other was a heavy-coated gelding. He choose this as the more likely of

92

the two to carry his weight.

Frome was fifty feet away when he detected movement in the pines on the rim across the valley. He bent in his saddle, reaching for his carbine. The movement became a shape. A horse and rider came slowly into view, turning downwards towards the grazing horses. The horses looked at the new intruder.

Frome swore softly. The rider – a small man or a boy – was also loosening rope. If the horses spooked, Frome knew that there was not enough left in the pony beneath him to overtake them.

Frome gestured, trying to turn the new arrival aside. He couldn't call for that would bolt the mustangs. The new arrival took no notice, but Frome saw that he had slowed his pony, and was carefully loosening his rope. At least, he looked experienced. Probably he wouldn't make his throw before Frome, but would wait and throw simultaneously. Then Frome had another grim thought. Supposing they both threw for the same mount?

Then a groan split from Frome's lips as he recognized the rider. It was no small man or boy; it was Curly. Wearing a rough range shirt, hat and denim trousers, a Winchester poking from her saddle bucket, Curly was moving in on the horses. Frome cursed. He thought: Spook those broncs, Curly, and I'll give you a hiding with your own rope.

Curly had obviously recognized him by now, but she gave no sign of recognition. She was watching the mustangs, hardly moving, stiff in her saddle.

The minutes passed as they pressed in at the stream from both sides. The mustangs were worried. No longer drinking, they had lifted heads, stood stiffly. It wouldn't take much to make them bolt.

Now Frome worried about which bronc Curly had selected. She hadn't made any mistakes up to now he conceded, but that didn't mean she had horse savvy. Ten to one, he thought, she throws for the gelding, fouls my line, and the broncs get clear. The gelding looked a handsome animal, and Frome hadn't known a woman yet who wasn't eventually cheated on a horse deal because she couldn't distinguish between a *handsome* horse and a good horse. Even Hesta put looks before stamina.

The gap closed. Now Curly was smiling at him. Frome's answer was a scowl. They were ten feet from the horses on either side. Frome lifted his rope slowly; Curly did likewise. Then Frome snapped, 'Now!'

The heads of the horses stiffened at the cry. Frome's rope snapped through air. And Curly's. The horses bunched, swerved, then bolted. Frome snagged the rope to his saddle horn and waited. Curly did the same. The ropes flipped up, tightened, became taut. Frome's horse dug its hoofs at the ground and took the weight.

The horses were up the slope. Then two of them went down, snapped back by the singing ropes. One was the gelding; the other the little paint pony. They hit the ground together, rolling, kicking up dirt. They came up and fought the rope, and then they relaxed, gave in, and Frome and Curly dragged them in.

Frome was out of the saddle, holding tightly on the rope and taking the headstraps from the spent pony. Curly did likewise. 'All right, Curly,' Frome said. 'You've made your point. You can rope. And you know horses. But as soon as you've switched saddles, you can hit back for Plattsville.'

She avoided that. She said sarcastically, 'I must say you

94

disappoint me, Dave. I thought you would have known more about horses. Yet you ignore the paint and rope the gelding. Obviously you are one of these many men who are fooled because a horse has good looks.'

Frome saw that Curly was laughing. 'I'll settle that argument another time. You head for Plattsville.'

'I can't do that. I'm heading for Denton. Of course . . . if you would rather ride alone.'

'Why Denton?' Frome got the headstraps on the mustang, and held the reins firmly while he removed the lariat from its neck and then switched blanket and saddle.

'I hear they need a good singer there.'

Frome shrugged. 'A poor excuse. Denton may need a singer but they don't rate one. It's a free country, but Denton's a long haul. I hope you can keep pace with me.'

'Seeing the horse you selected,' she smiled, 'I don't think I'll have any difficulty.'

Frome said, 'So you think. That paint will be bones when this gelding's still walking.'

'About what all the gelding can do – walk.'

Curly finished saddling the paint as Frome swung into the saddle of the gelding, and started up the valley without looking back. She overtook him at the rim. Frome said, 'I didn't know you knew so much about horses. Where did you learn it?'

'Kansas Flats. It's a little place a hundred miles beyond Dodge.'

'I think I've heard of it,' Frome said. 'My father had a horse outfit just outside Dodge. What's the rest of your name, Curly, I might know your kin?'

'Peterson. My real name's Julia Peterson.'

Frome thought a moment. 'Can't say I've heard of

THE KANSAS FAST GUN

Petersons that way.'

Curly smiled. 'That makes us even. I can't remember hearing of the name of Frome. We couldn't have had famous families.'

'Let's ride,' Frome said, jacking the gelding forward. Curly spurred the paint. They thundered through the belly-high grama grass, sending steers fanning out on either side of them.

Beyond a grass ridge seven miles on, Frome's land began.

But his home range was a further ten miles on, and Frome was aiming for home, for it was only there that he could be certain of finding fresh mounts to continue his ride through the Arrows.

Curly kept up the mile-eating gait. The little paint never more than a horse's length behind the tall gelding.

It was dark when they urged their spent ponies up a hummock a mile away from the Broken Arrow headquarters valley. The gelding was snorting, spilling saliva. With every step, Frome now expected it to fold beneath him.

He tried as much as possible to keep the horse to the down-grades. The worst had happened. Frome hadn't found any more wandering remuda broncs in the grass ocean. He realized now that the prairies had certainly been combed by the Double Star, gathering in all the ponies they could for the coming troubles.

Curly swung the little paint, which was in better condition, beside Frome. 'Switch mounts, Dave. You take the paint.'

Frome said, 'Not a hope, kid. He might fold any

minute. I don't want you to be beneath him.'

'But he'll carry my weight better.'

Frome said, 'If he folds, I know I can spring free. I don't know if you can do it.'

They had covered another half a mile before the gelding gave in. Stopping stiff-legged, it refused to go further. Frome decided the animal had given its best. He swung from the saddle, began to strip the headgear and saddle from it.

Curly looked down from her saddle, a black shape beneath the curtain of stars. Frome took off the gear and swung the gelding towards water, slapping it.

'I'll carry your saddle,' Curly said.

'Not necessary,' Frome said, 'I'm leaving it here.'

Frome unstrapped the bucketed rifle, left the saddle, and began to walk. Curly dismounted and led the paint, walking beside him.

Twenty minutes later, without a word being exchanged, they topped the valley rim, pushed through timber on the rim, and looked down on Frome's headquarters.

Curly saw the lighted cabin as Frome gripped her, moving her back.

'There's a light in my cabin,' Frome said. 'Can't be any of my boys. They're working for Glinton.'

Curly watched him drag the Winchester free from the bucket. Then he was moving forward, crouched, dodging from tree to tree. 'Be careful, Dave,' Curly called softly.

Only the slight murmur of the night breeze in the trees answered her.

CHAPTER 13

Picking his way carefully through the brush on the slope, Frome worked his way down to the floor of the valley. He reached it and hunkered down. He noticed that no light showed from the bunkhouse or the cookshack. A glance at the corral was rewarding. Two black shapes were by the poles – saddled ponies, ready to go.

Frome levered a bullet into the Winchester, advanced across the clearing in a crouch, moving straight for the cabin. Reaching the veranda rail, and noticing that the door was closed, he swung round to the side wall, eased himself up and looked through the window.

Two men were in the main room, and he recognized them both. His lips tightened. Particularly, he recognized the man in the buckskin jacket. Buckskin was sprawled across Frome's couch, his arm heavily bandaged and tucked in a fold of the jacket. Then Frome hadn't been wrong; he had winged the man as he'd been galloping for cover behind the outcropping.

The other man, tall, heavily built, stood by the fireplace. He looked angry about something. The wounded man raised his arm, said bitterly, 'I tell you, Harry, I can't take it.'

The standing man snapped: 'And I tell you, you've got to.'

'But the pain's awful. Let me rest. At least until sun-up.'

The man moved in on him, scowling. 'You're not going to die, Dirk. It's only a bullet wound, and I've cleaned it.'

'But you ain't got the pain to ride with. I've got it!'

'Sure you've got pain. That was a rifle bullet!'

'So let me rest a little,' the man whined. 'Only until daylight.'

'I tell you, we can't take the chance. Frome's on the prod, we didn't get him. And we ain't only got Frome to worry about now.'

The wounded man snarled. 'Frome! We were sure wrong about him. I thought I'd seen him somewheres before. Up Dodge way. But the name Frome don't register. Yeah, Bennett was wrong about him. He's one of them Kansas fast guns, that's for sure.'

'So,' the standing man snarled, 'do you want him round your neck again? And what about Bennett? He won't only be mad because we didn't get Frome. He's going to hate our guts to killing point because we've rolled off some of Frome's stock. He wants Frome dead; and Frome'll soon be dead, so Bennett's already looking on Broken Arrow stock as his own. We stay here and both Frome and Bennett stand a chance to get us. We've got to leave right now and get to Five Mile Canyon ready to move out with the herd and the rest of the boys.'

'I know that, Harry, but my arm. I'm not going to be any help to you unless I rest my arm.'

The standing man scowled. 'You aren't no Breslow. You aren't a patch on any of your brothers. Blacky'll sure be sick of you. And you don't measure up to Pa.'

The man on the couch laughed derisively. 'Pa weren't so hot. Got himself lynched, didn't he?' He bent forward. 'Now be a good big brother and get me some more of that coffee.'

'The pot's empty. I'll have to go to the shack and make some more. You'll get your coffee, Dirk. But be ready to ride after it.'

Frome saw the big man pick up a coffee pot and move to the door. He came round the veranda rail, hefting the Winchester, crouched by the steps.

He knew the Breslows by reputation. They were notorious around Kansas City. It looked then as if he was about to end Kansas City's troubles. He felt an excitement. Then Kyle Bennett was behind the attempt on his life, and his theory that Bennett had been behind all the troubles was confirmed.

The door opened. Frome saw Harry Breslow in the doorway. Frome reversed the rifle. He wanted these jiggers alive. Breslow moved forward to the step. As Breslow stepped down, so Frome came up. The stock of the carbine swung up, zipping. It hit Breslow squarely in the face with a meaty smack and the snap of nose bone. The man fell face forward off the step, a groan bursting from his lips.

Frome stepped over him, stood the rifle by the rail, lifted his right Colt.

Dirk Breslow's voice reached him. 'What in hell Harry was that?'

The boards creaked beneath Frome as he crossed to the door.

Breslow snarled, 'Harry?'

Frome bent to the floor, peeped into the room, wanting

100

to take Dirk Breslow alive. Breslow was jittery now, and he whipped up his Colt in a swift movement. He said nervously, 'Harry?'

Frome said, 'Harry dropped out. Throw out your gun, Dirk, and save yourself some grief.'

Dirk Breslow moved. He threw himself sideways off the couch, fell heavily to the floor and rolled away. Frome could no longer see him. A slug tore a chip from the door jamb and whined into the night.

'Frome!' he snarled.

'That's right. Now toss out your irons.'

Breslow laughed hysterically. 'So you can take me to the hangman? After what we did to Grape and Taber, you won't give us a chance.'

Frome knew it all now. 'I can understand why you want me dead, Dirk, but why Grape and Taber?'

'That wasn't my fault, Frome,' Breslow said anxiously, 'honest. That was a mistake. The boys knew Grape, but they didn't know you. Taber fitted your description. It was dark. Even Farrow was fooled.'

Frome thought that that looked right. Taber was of the same build and colouring as himself. 'OK, so throw out your irons.'

'Listen, Frome, you've got to give me a break, see.'

'I'm counting to three, Dirk. If you haven't thrown up by then, I'm going to swing and pump a shot into Harry's head.'

'Go ahead, Frome. He's the one you want. He's the one that gunned Matt Grape and Taber.'

Frome swung up. He said, 'One'; he stepped back. 'Two'; and then he sprang back off the porch, darted round the rail, and came up at the window. But Breslow had anticipated him. A shot sounded in the room. Glass pinged. The light went out. Frome fired three shots into the room, aiming for the spot where he guessed Breslow might be. Then he swung back around the cabin and dropped by the veranda rail.

He listened, heard no movement. 'If you're not out in five seconds, Dirk, I'm going to fire the cabin.'

Breslow said hysterically: 'You wouldn't fire your own property?' But Frome could tell that the desperado believed it.

'I'd still show a profit,' he answered, 'if I caught a rat like you.'

Breslow said, 'If I come out, what'll you do?'

'Pass you over to the law.'

'That's a promise – you'll hand Harry and me over?'

'You have my word.'

A pause. A snarl. 'OK, Frome, you win. I'm throwing out my iron.'

'Both of them,' Frome snapped. 'and make sure the hammers are down.'

Breslow snarled. 'You won't give a man opportunity to bring off a million-to-one chance.'

Frome stepped back off the veranda. 'That's right.'

There came a metallic thump. Then another. The guns hit the boards of the veranda. Frome said, 'Come on out, with your good hand high.' Breslow appeared in the doorway, stepped forward off the step. Frome checked that he was carrying no sneak gun, then pushed him towards the corral.

Curly came across the clearing, her carbine hanging by her side. Frome took a rope from one of the ponies and began to tie Breslow to the poles. He went back for Harry

102

Breslow, and roped him upright beside his brother.

'You ain't going to keep us standing all night, Frome?' Dirk Breslow snapped.

'I sure am,' Frome said.

Frome took Curly to the cabin, got a lamp from the bedroom and lit it. Curly looked around the long room with interest. She saw the mess the Breslows had made and the broken glass. 'I'll clear this up.'

Frome said, 'It'll keep.'

But Curly, ignoring that, began to straighten things. Frome sat on the couch, began to roll a cigarette. He was thinking. The Breslows had driven his beef to the Five Mile Canyon, thirty miles away from Denton.

If he took a shortcut through the Arrows and turned right from Denton, he would arrive at the O Diamond spread, which was not far from the canyon. He could rely on old Jacob Haines and the O Diamond crew for support, particularly as the Breslows had stolen O Diamond broncs. If he went on to Denton, it would take him thirty miles away from the canyon, and then he would have to go into detail with Marshal Keester. Keester was a fast man of action when convinced, but he had a bigger bone in his head than most men, and needed some convincing.

He saw what the Breslows had been up to. They had been brought in for one job by Kyle Bennett – to nail Frome. But, realizing there was no opposition – for Frome should have died in the hotel – they had decided to drive off a herd of Broken Arrow prime beef and thus in a way double cross Bennett. They could have been across the border into Kansas, with their cattle sold, long before Bennett realized what had happened. And some fifteen thousand dollars was much more than Bennett was scheduled to pay them for killing Frome.

Frome got up, saw Curly busy straightening bric-a-brac on the desk. 'Forget that, Curly, let's get over to the cookshack and eat.'

Curly followed him. Frome stopped by the corral rail. He said:

'Where's your big brother Blacky Breslow?'

Dirk Breslow said, 'He wasn't along on this caper.'

'Who's herding the cattle then that you've had driven to Five Mile Canyon?'

'You know that?' Dirk Breslow snarled.

'I overheard it. I reckon Blacky will be in charge of that. You're hoping that Blacky'll get free so that he can maybe shake you and Harry out of the Plattsville jail. Well, stop kidding yourself. How many men has Blacky got with him?'

'You'll never know; and you'll never get him.'

'Wishful thinking, Dirk.' Frome led Curly to the cookhouse. The Breslows had started the cookfire and water was on the boil. Frome made coffee, and Curly found bread, biscuits and new-fangled apple pie in Long Will's store.

They ate in silence. When he had finished and was rolling a cigarette, Frome said, 'I've got a problem. I've got a tough ride ahead of me over narrow hill trails. I know the way, so I should make out. But you'll have to stay behind, Curly.' He looked at her. 'I hate to leave you alone with those thugs out there.'

She said, 'I can take care of myself. I'm good with the Winchester.'

'OK, but don't listen to anything from those Breslows. They're desperate. They'll hang and they know it. You'll lock yourself in the cabin and stay there.'

She smiled wryly at the firmness in his voice. 'You make it sound like an order.'

Frome said harshly, 'It is an order.'

She smiled again. Frome got up, moved to the door, collecting some ropes on the way. 'I'll tie the Breslows good and tight. Only thing, you're not to go near them. Not even to give them a drink, you understand?'

'I understand, Dave.'

The softness in her voice made him swing towards her. He smiled down at her, took her in his arms, and kissed her. 'It's only that I want you safe, Curly. You know that?'

She nodded. She allowed him to kiss her again, and then she broke away. He led the way out of the shack. 'Now get to the cabin and lock yourself in. Knowing Long Will, he should be back by noon tomorrow. Nothing can keep him away from his kitchen for long.'

Curly crossed to the cabin. Frome watched her go, then went to the corral. He put an extra rope on each man, and checked that the knots were tight. He went across the cabin, retrieved the dropped Winchester, and looked at Curly as she stood in the doorway, the light behind her. 'See you tomorrow, Curly,' he whispered.

'Yes,' she answered. She went into the cabin, then closed and locked the door.

Frome went back to the saddled ponies at the corral, selected the best one, took a carbine from the saddle bucket, and pushed the new Winchester there. He dumped the carbine in the barn, crossed to where Dirk Breslow was roped. His handgun flashed into his hand and swung upwards. 'Don't want you annoying the lady, Dirk,' he said. And he laid the barrel across Breslow's skull. The man groaned and his head fell forward.

Frome swung into the saddle of the sorrel he had selected and swung it out of the valley, heading for the dim line of the Arrows.

CHAPTER 14

Frome pushed a little shaggy mountain pony over a hump on the Arrow trail and saw Denton laid out on a carpet of grass fifteen miles along the prairie to his left. He had made good time after switching from the spent sorrel to one of old John Chiswick's mountain ponies on the slopes of the hills.

He jerked the pony to a stop and, cocking a leg over the saddle horn and looking across at Denton, he built a smoke. Smoke spiralled from one chimney in the village. The black drape of night still curtained half the sky.

Frome smoked the cigarette, and rubbed his face, fighting off the urge for sleep. Then he started the pony moving down the narrow track for the prairie floor. Two miles down, the trail widened out and sank beneath a covering of timber. Frome pushed through the timber, finding narrow trails, and finally reached flat O Diamond graze.

It was getting on towards seven o'clock and the sun was a half disc on the horizon rim, when he splashed across a creek and came up into sight of the O Diamond headquarters. The day was just beginning on the horse ranch, and several men were washing in a large tub outside the bunkhouse.

The sound of Frome's approach brought old Jacob Haines to the door of the cabin, and the men swinging from the tub. Haines came towards him, his wrinkled face splittering into laughter. Dismounting, Frome extended his hand and shook the old man's.

'Long time no see, Dave. What's brought you this way?'

Frome said, 'This isn't a social call. You lost any stock, Jake?'

The old man stepped back, anger showing in his eyes. 'Have I lost stock! Lost eleven horses I'd saddle broken three days ago from a meadow less than a mile away. Why, do you know something?'

Frome said he knew something. Haines grabbed his arm, leading him to the ranchhouse. 'Let's talk about it, Dave.' He raised his voice. 'Ma. We got a visitor – Dave Frome!'

Frome entered the long, log-beamed cabin. Several of the hands were already seated at a table. Ma Haines poked her head from a kitchen and greeted Frome. The rancher smelt frying eggs and bacon and boiling coffee.

Haines guided Frome to the table. He sat opposite, hawked forward, eager to hear the details. Frome told him everything, even mentioning that Kyle Bennett was behind it. The crew crowded into the cabin, forming a circle around them. Jacob Haines slammed the table. 'What are we waiting for, let's ride?'

Frome said, 'There isn't any hurry. The boys in the canyon won't move off until Harry and Dirk Breslow return. And they can't know yet that I've taken the Breslows and killed the rest of the gang they sent to

Plattsville to get me.'

'Huh-huh!' Haines said. 'How many do you reckon there are?'

'Can't be many left,' Frome said. He looked around, counting. Including Haines, his sons, and himself, they were eight strong. 'I reckon we should outnumber them by two to one.'

'We know where they're at, and we know the Five Mile Canyon like the backs of our hands,' Haines said. He thumped the table impatiently. 'Let's saddle up.'

With the smell of the breakfast cooking, Frome felt his hunger. Ma Haines came out of the kitchen. 'Hold on, Jake,' she snapped. 'Mister Frome'll be hungry. And you can't expect the boys to ride well on empty stomachs.'

Haines conceded that by wagging his head. He began to talk about Kyle Bennett's plan. 'Hell, I've never heard of a steal that big before. What in darnation is the world coming to?'

Frome said, 'When you lost your horses, didn't you check the canyon?'

Haines answered. 'No, the sign read they all went the other way. We followed them for twenty miles on past Denton before we lost the sign. They must've doubled back over a hundred miles.'

Ma Haines brought platters of steaming eggs and bacon to the table. She served Frome and Haines first. Then the rest of the crew squatted round the table. Haines ate quickly, chewing and talking at the same time. He had never thought much of Kyle Bennett because of the manner in which the boy had deserted the breed woman at Denton. 'I don't begrudge a man his woman if he so fancies, but he's got to care for her.'

109

Haines cleared his plate first. Still eating and ignoring his wife's pleading that he should watch his digestion, he stomped across to a guns rack and lifted down an old Henry. He checked the load, strapped on a gunbelt, then began to cram cartridges into his pocket. 'As soon as we've left, ma, you hitch up the team and head to Denton. Tell Keester to get out to the canyon with a posse. Warn him that if he's slow in arriving, I'll deal with any of the rustlers I catch alive. He'll have a lynching then to explain away.' Haines smiled. 'That'll shift him.'

When a couple of the boys had nearly cleared their plates, Haines snapped, 'You've eaten enough. Go and cut out the best broncs in the corrals.'

When Frome had finished his meal and exchanged news with Mrs Haines, fresh horses were in the yard, and all of the boys were armed. They swung into saddles, old Haines lifted his hat to his wife, and they swung out of the yard across the creek and curved left.

They galloped for six miles across grasslands which were only sparsely timbered, pushed through a stand of ragged juniper, and reached badlands, mile after mile of rock and sandy waste. Ahead of them, a jutting of the Arrows, was the Five Mile Canyon.

Frome could see that it was an ideal place to hide stolen stock. From its towering rim, a sentry could observe the country for miles around. He guessed that they had already been spotted, but Haines had expected and made plans for that. To put the sentry off, Haines swung the group hard right, leading them to cedar thickets which rolled up the slopes of the Arrows and away from the frontal entrance to the canyon.

Watching from above, the rustler lookout would believe

110

that the O Diamond crew were combing the cedar thickets for wandered stock. To implant the idea further in the sentry's mind, Haines gave a signal when the crew were a mile off the timbered slopes, and they fanned out.

They hit the brush and disappeared in a tangle of undergrowth. Following Haines, Frome smashed through creeper, arm raised to stop branches from striking his face. Some of the boys found wild broncs and flushed them out into the open. But they all kept moving to the left. Eventually they linked up, following a narrow trail in single file.

'There isn't a lot of time,' Jake Haines observed. 'That lookout will wonder what's happened to us in a while. Old Lady Luck might be on our side, though. These rustlers mightn't know that there's a slit entrance to the canyon this way.' He spat into a chokeberry bush. 'It narrows to nothing nearly and is thickly overgrowed. We'll have to funnel through for a spell single file.'

The brush cleared ahead and Frome saw the stream. Beyond the creek he saw the canyon wall. They crossed the creek, allowing the horses a drink, then pushed on, Jake Haines out in front, studying the canyon face. Haines twisted suddenly. 'Hear that in the distance, Dave?' Frome could hear nothing. 'Your cattle bawling. They know pappy's coming for them!'

Frome smiled. They began to climb. Then Frome saw the crevice in the canyon wall which was almost hidden by a tangle of brush. Haines swung. 'Single file until it widens. Then we bunch up and hit the canyon basin at a gallop. The way I figure it, these rustlers'll have their camp on a shelf more'n halfway down, facing the other way. When we spot it, we swing in, bounce off our ponies and start up the sides. If they're more'n we can handle, just pin 'em down and wait for Keester to arrive. That sound OK to you, Dave?'

Frome nodded. Haines spat, hefted his Henry from his saddle bucket, and swung his pony up to the crevice. Frome took next place, lifting out his Winchester. They followed a narrow track between the towering walls for some fifty yards. Then Frome noticed the canyon wall lifted higher and also the trail widened.

Another fifty yards and it had widened so much that they could travel four abreast. Then suddenly the basin opened before them, and Frome could hear the cattle clearly. Jake Haines raised his rifle above his head and snapped, 'Let's ride 'em!'

It started as a trot, went into a canter as the canyon opened, then became a mad gallop as they hit the basin floor and widened out; eight riders, strung out, low in the saddle, hefting Winchesters, Spencers and Henrys, and yelling at the top of their voices.

The first thing Frome saw were his cattle grazing near a stream on the right of the basin. Next he spotted the rustlers' camp, high in the rocks as Haines said it would be, where a tell-tale whiff of fire smoke pinpointed it. Dark against the grey and yellow rock, he could see men hurrying for cover.

Looking upwards to the rim, where the sentry might be posted, Frome saw sun flash on gun barrel. He judged that the man had one of them in his sights and was about to press the trigger. Several shots cracked out seconds later, and gunsmoke whipped up from the rustlers' camp as the breeze caught it. The canyon walls took up the sound and multiplied it. Mushrooms of dust kicked up around the fast moving horses as the carbine bullets thudded into the ground. Just to the left of Frome, a pony took a slug in the head, turned a somersault over its head, sent a rider thumping to the ground.

They were curving in now, racing for the brush-covered slopes just to the left and below the camp.

Frome snatched his legs from the stirrups as the pony raced for the climb, then jack-knifed up and rolled from the bronc's back. The ground rushed up, clouted him viciously, then he was scrambling for cover, his rifle lifted.

He hit the slope and flattened as a slug sent shale spitting at him. He scrambled on, moving for an arch of rocks. The sound of carbine bullets and galloping ponies seemed to be all around him. Reaching it, he looked back and saw a half a dozen riderless ponies turning away from the wall. Just below him, Jake Haines had hit dirt. The old man, now smiling, began to follow him. Here and there, Frome could see the rest of the O Diamond boys hunkering down or scrambling for cover.

Frome reached the rock formation, bellied down, poked the carbine through a groove and fired off a shot into the rock cluster above. He jacked the guard, fired again. Haines dropped beside him, kicking up grit.

Haines said: 'They're well fortified. This could be a long siege.'

Frome said, 'I don't know about that. They've got so much rock around them, that it could mean their death. Look, Jake, at the way the rock face just above them curves under.'

Haines said, 'I see it.' Then he chuckled. 'I see what you mean. But we'd need to be a bit higher.'

'Then let's get weaving.'

They came up together, began to run up the slope. The heavy climb exhausted them, brought the sweat to their hands and faces. Dust came up beneath their bodies, pinpointing them for the rustlers. Slugs ripped into the brush around them. Heavy firing came from beneath them as the O Diamond boys fired from cover. Then Frome reached an outcropping, dropped, poked his gaze over the top, saw the way the enemy stronghold sat, and grunted with satisfaction. Haines dropped breathless beside him.

He said, 'This is just right, Dave. We'll cut 'em to pieces.'

They poked their carbines over the rockrim, aiming for the fall-away rock, and began firing. The bullets tore at the rock surface, and ricocheted into the camp with whining sounds. Frome kept pumping the shots at the rock from his thirteen-shot Winchester. He saw chips spindle out from the wall, tearing at the unprotected backs of the rustlers, and judged that most of the slugs would be bouncing that way.

Now the rest of the O Diamond boys got the idea. Instead of aiming slugs at the rocks behind which the desperadoes sheltered – slugs which bounced back on the slope – they aimed for the wall behind.

Frome judged that there had been four men firing from the camp, and another – the lookout – from the rockrim. But firing soon tapered off from the camp when Frome and the O Diamond men pumped ricocheting shells into the camp at fifty per minute.

Frome pushed thirteen fresh slugs into his carbine, and fired them off at the rock in as many seconds. And then Haines shouted above the snarl of shot and tortured metal that the rustlers weren't firing any more. Frome got a vivid imagined picture of the survivors clawing among the rocks, looking for protection from the bouncing shells and rock splinter.

Frome said, 'You'd better move in on it with your boys. I'm going after that sonofabitch on the rim.'

Haines grunted, came up, springing over the rock and waving his men on. Frome moved also, zig-zagging up the slope, racing for the canyon rim. He passed beyond the camp. He was within yards of the canyon roof, and then shots began to groove into the rocks around him. Rock splinter razored his cheek, brought the warm blood to his face. Another bullet gouged up dust between his scissoring feet. Frome pointed his carbine up, but the sun was too bright over the rim, blinding him. He realized that he was a sitting duck. He realized that the next rifle bullet could shatter him, and send him skidding down the slope.

He fired then, aiming his shots for a blurred line where he imagined the rim to be. He fired once, then he fired again. He hammered off his shells until the Winchester was empty. Then, dropping it, he lifted a Colt, fanned the hammer, emptying the gun along the rim. No more shots came. He pouched the sixgun, and began to climb again. Weaving for the top, clutching at rough brush and slippery rock, anything which touched his searching hands. The sun still dazzled him.

He hit the rim at last, folding over it, bringing up his other Colt. He got a momentary impression of a beard-visored face above a rock formation. A bullet cut air inches from his face. Frome punched off two shots at the rocks, then brought his legs over the rim and rolled for cover.

Silence. Had he hit the man? Too much to hope for, he thought. Better to be safe than sorry. He lay tight against

115

the sun-hot rock, pushing fresh shells from his belt into both Colts. The sound of sporadic firing came up from the slope below. Frome thought grimly that Jake Haines would be finishing off the rustlers. He knew Jake's philosophy. Why keep the poor critters about when they had to hang eventually anyway? That was the way Jake thought. Best get it over with. A bullet's quicker than the rope. Be merciful and finish it right away.

Frome moved then, bellying out across the flat rock for cover nearer to the rock formation. He was inches from the rock when sunlight touched on steel. Two bullets screeched off rock inches from him. Frome fired, moved for cover. Again silence, but he knew the sentry was still alive, and knew where he was. But how to reach him? He took a quick look over the rocks, and saw that the ground between him and the ridge was crinkled and pitted. Further over to the right, great slashes and shallows bisected the ground. Frome rolled over and away. He began to wriggle to the right of the sentry's position.

He reached a groove deep enough to hold him in cover. He rolled into it. Then he began to move along it. It turned sharply and he saw that it would take him right along the rock formation, but on the opposite side to the sentry.

Now the shallow deepened as the granite ledge which was the beginning of the rock formation began on his right. He moved more quickly now. The formation climbed until it was three-feet above Frome and, on the otherside somewhere, the sentry waited. But where? It was almost comic. Had the rustler moved in the direction from which Frome had just come, was he moving in the opposite direction, or was he level with Frome, only a few feet of rock between them?

Frome decided to find out. He lifted a cartridge from his belt, and flicked it over to the right. It clanked on rock. Less than a yard from him, the beard-blackened face appeared behind a long Colt's barrel, and fired off two slugs in the direction of the sound. Frome levelled his Colt, fired, and the Colt span from the man's hand, driven by the smack of the bullet. The man came up, screaming at the pain that laced his arm, his fingers clawing.

Frome came up, stepping over the rocks, jacking back the hammer, levelling on the man.

'You lousy, two-faced, belly-crawling, skunk's son. . . .' The man snarled flipping his hand. Frome saw his right holster was empty; his left still carried a Colt. The likeness of the man to Harry and Dirk Breslow was unmistakable. This man was taller, leaner, tougher, more intelligent. His dark eyes, twin diamonds of hate, flicked over Frome, and he cursed him again.

Frome said, 'Cut the parlour talk. You must be Blacky Breslow?'

He looked surprised at that, never having met Frome before. 'How did you guess?'

'I heard a conversation between your brothers and Kyle Bennett,' Frome lied. 'Bennett was about to string 'em up. Dirk blabbed out the whole story of how you hijacked Frome's cattle.'

The man's hard lips tightened. 'You're a liar! They had no quarrel with Kyle!'

'But Kyle had plenty with them. It wasn't so much the cattle rustle that annoyed Kyle as the fact that your brothers failed to get Frome. Kyle thought they might've done a deal with Frome. Anyway, they were too talkative.

117

So he hanged them.'

The man looked at Frome through slitted, suspicious eyes. 'You're lying,' he said again, but Frome could see that Blacky Breslow half believed him.

'All right, I'm lying. So how did I get here? So how did I know you had the cattle in this canyon, or that you were Blacky Breslow? I'm telling you, Dirk broke down, he blabbed it all. Then Kyle swung him and Harry on a cotton-wood on Frome's place.'

'Who are you?'

'I'm Kyle's righthand. Does my name matter?'

Bitterness showed on Blacky Breslow's face. His face became hooded. He forgot the pain in his hand as he pictured the death of his brothers swinging on a thick cottonwood tree . . . ending just like their father had ended. His voice was muffled when he spoke. 'How . . . how could they miss Frome? He was easy; he was a gun-shy; and there were five of them? Dirk's never been much, but Harry was always a smart boy.'

'Just one of those things. Me, I don't know. Kyle doesn't. But they missed him, and he dropped three of your help, including a kid named Farrow.'

Breslow lifted his head suddenly, and tensed. His left hand dropped, inches from his Colt.

Frome said, 'Don't try it.'

'Why not. Bennett and Speakman don't want me alive; not after they've killed my brothers. You've been sent to finish me, so don't deny it. But I've got a chance . . . I've got a chance to beat you to the draw, get away from your gunslingers down there . . . and go after Bennett and Speakman.'

Frome had learned for the first time that Bennett and

Speakman were in this thing together. He didn't want Breslow to go for his gun yet. He wanted to keep him talking.

'Speakman?' Frome said, 'Speakman wasn't in on the lynching.'

Breslow shrugged. 'So what, he's a partner with Bennett in this deal, ain't he?'

Frome took a chance. He said, 'That's news to me.'

Breslow smiled savagely at that. 'I see. Kyle never did trust anybody. So he didn't confide in you . . . well . . . just in case you beat me, feller . . . I'll tell you the story. If Bennett didn't tell you, it means he doesn't trust you. Maybe what I tell you will do Bennett some harm someday . . . that's if you beat me to the draw.'

Frome said, 'I'm listening.'

'Speakman and Bennett arranged the deal in Kansas City three months ago. They'd start a fake war between ranchers and miners, get a few on both sides killed off, and the leaders like Glinton Le Roy, his son Denny, and Frome. Then Bennett as kin to Le Roy would take over the management of the Double Star and Broken Arrow ranges and probably get them eventually by marrying Hesta Le Roy, who was his old sweetheart.'

Frome said, 'I see, but what would Speakman get from the deal?'

Breslow said, 'A free hand to mine in the hills.'

'There's only one snag,' Frome said, 'the range wouldn't be any good to Bennett if he couldn't get clear water from the hills.'

'They even worked that out,' Breslow said. 'Speakman sent an engineer down to make tests. There's water not too far down in many parts of the grasslands on that side of the Arrows.'

Breslow smiled slowly. He could see that Frome was interested. He misunderstood the man's interest. 'If you live, then, you ought to be able to make some use of that . . . to Bennett's cost of course.'

Frome only nodded. He saw the gleam that came into Breslow's eyes. He lifted the Colt on the man. 'I've got you covered, Breslow; I shouldn't try it.'

'Can't you give a guy an even break? Holster that iron. Let's draw together.'

Frome said, 'Not a chance.'

Breslow snapped, 'Then I'll make one.' His left-hand flashed for his gun. Frome saw it blurr, lifting the heavy Colt from leather; then Frome snapped the hammer forward on the Colt, driving a slug at Breslow's wrist. The bullet cut deeply into skin, not touching bone. The Colt dropped from Breslow's hand. The damaged wrist went to his mouth as he tried to stop the flow of blood.

Jacob Haines came over the rim with three of his boys.

Breslow looked from them to Frome, then said, 'OK, finish it.'

Frome said, 'You helped me. You'll go to jail. You'll stand trial for rustling only. I'll see to that.'

Breslow snapped. 'That was fancy shooting, feller. Who are you?'

Frome holstered his Colt. 'A gun-shy named Dave Frome.'

CHAPTER 15

It was late evening and dark when Frome put the pony over the rim into his home valley. He jerked the pony to a stop, hawking forward in his saddle, lips tightening. No light showed in the cabin; and he saw the black shapes of the Breslows bent stiff and grotesquely forward against the ropes that lashed them to the corral poles. Frome swung from the saddle, dragging the rifle from his boot with the same movement. He hurried down the track without caution, thinking only of Curly.

Reaching the corral, he dropped by the poles. He looked to the brothers. There was no doubt about it. Both were dead. Long dead. He could even see the blood glisten on their shirtfronts. He found his hands were sweating as he slick-slacked a shell into the Winchester. He moved towards the cabin. Throwing all caution to the wind, he shouted Curly's name.

And then her voice reached him clearly from the cabin. She opened the door. She put her rifle down and hurried towards him. He went to meet her, propped the Winchester by the veranda and took her in his arms.

Then she told him, with the horror twisting her

features, of the death of the Breslows, killed by Bennett and a bunch of men. 'It happened just before noon. I heard horsemen coming, and ducked out of the cabin and hid on the slopes. There were a dozen of them – and Bennett, the man you fought in Plattsville. The Breslows tried to talk to him, but he was angry, he wouldn't listen. He opened fire.'

She broke down, weeping before she could finish it. Frome lifted her into his arms and carried her into the cabin. He went out, collected his rifle, returned to the cabin, closed the door and lit the lamp.

Curly began to tell it again, going into more details. Bennett was like a mad man, she said. 'He had cursed the Breslows for not killing you, for mistaking Dwight Taber for you, and then for stealing your cattle. Dirk Breslow tried to argue, pleaded, but Bennett wouldn't listen. Then he gave the order.' Curly stopped.

Curly said that the dozen or so men, laughing and swearing, had opened fire, emptying their guns into the brothers. One of the men had then searched the buildings. Bennett had rejected a suggestion that they should try and follow the sign left by the rustled cattle. Frome was still alive, he had said, so they were still his cattle. He had also rejected a suggestion that two men should wait in the valley in case Frome returned. Bennett had said that it would take more than two men to trap Frome like that, and that in any case, Frome would be on the other side of the Arrows, trailing the rustlers. They had then ridden away.

Frome told Curly what had happened at the Five Mile Canyon, that Blacky Breslow had talked before enough witnesses to get court convictions against Bennett and

Speakman for murder and conspiracy.

He smiled softly, 'Now all we've got to do is catch the pair so they can stand trial.'

Curly said, 'And that won't be easy.'

'They have a hardcase crew of some fifty men,' Frome answered. 'No, it won't be easy.' Frome got up. 'I'll make some coffee. You sit tight, keep your senses trained for sound. Bennett might come back.'

Frome went across to the cookhouse, lit the stove, found water and put it on to boil. Then he freed the bodies of the Breslows from the ropes which held them, covered them with sacking, and carried them to the barn. He brought his own pony down from the valley rim, watered it, and placed it beside the pony which was already saddled. Curly and he might need the ponies in a hurry.

He returned to the cookshack, washed himself, and then made coffee. When he reached the cabin with coffee and food, Curly had relaxed and was seated on the couch. While eating, he noticed that Curly had cleaned the place up. He thanked her, and it reminded her of something.

She frowned, put down her plate, went to the mantelpiece and returned with a large gold watch. 'While cleaning up, I found this, Dave.'

Frome said, 'So, what's the problem? That was my father's.'

Still puzzled, she opened the back, and showed him the photograph of a family group there. It was the picture of a father, a mother, and three sons, and it had been taken many years before.

'That's my father,' Frome explained, 'and the little kid with the sour expression is me.'

'But,' Curly said, 'it says at the bottom "The Morgan

123

family – Dodge City"?'

Frome said, 'I see. Well, my real name is Morgan. I'll have to tell you about it.'

Curly sprang up, backed away from him, and horror showed on her face. She said accusingly, 'Then you're David Morgan?'

Frome felt a chill climb his spine. 'That's – that's right. . . .' Curly still backed away from him. She crushed her hand against her mouth suddenly and tears appeared on her cheeks. 'Then you're the Dave Morgan who shot my fiancé on Front Street in Dodge six years ago!'

Horrified, remembering the Stuart boy he had killed, Frome moved towards her.

'Don't come near me,' she screamed, 'don't touch me!'

Frome stopped paralysed. There was a long silence. Then the rain began to beat on the roof with a monotonous sound. Frome turned, moved across the room, and stood by the window, watching the heavy rain drip down the panes.

He was still standing there minutes later when the sound of horsemen approaching reached him.

He hurried to the lamp, turned it out, snatched up his carbine, and raced back to the window.

CHAPTER 16

Frome dragged back the curtaining, yelled to Curly to take cover, and triggered a shell into the carbine. Rain lashed the window, glistening, running down the panes in rivulets. A point of fork lightning jagged down beyond the valley's rim, and for a fraction of a second Frome saw the horsemen swing in around the corral. Their faces were hidden by pulled down hatbrims, their bodies shapeless in shiny slickers. They formed up before the veranda, and one dismounted. 'You there, Dave?' he called.

Frome, recognizing Sam Justin's voice, lowered the rifle. 'Here, Sam. Curly, put the lamp on.' He moved to the door and opened it. The light bubbled on behind him, chasing the shadows from the long room. Justin, without shape in the long slicker, stepped into the room. Now other men dismounted and followed him in. Frome recognized their faces.

'This is it,' Justin said grimly. 'The showdown. Glinton Le Roy's been killed. Kyle Bennett killed him.'

Frome, remembering what Breslow had told him, only

125

nodded. Justin continued, 'And Bennett and Speakman have linked forces. They know they're up against it. They're going to make one last attempt to clear the Arrows of ranches . . . or go under in the attempt. We're marshalling all the men we can at the Double Star.'

Frome said, 'What happened to Glinton?'

Justin explained. Glinton Le Roy had been sleeping badly since the death of Denny. Apparently he had heard Bennett leave the house in the early hours of the morning after receiving a signal – pebbles thrown against the window. Le Roy must have followed Bennett, heard him conferring with somebody who had brought him news from town – probably the news that five hundred head of Frome's cattle had been rustled. Le Roy had heard too much. Either he betrayed his presence, or openly challenged Bennett. There was a shot. When people came running, Bennett had said that he thought he had seen an intruder and fired at him. Nobody had missed Glinton at that time, had believed Bennett and returned to their beds. Bennett had moved swiftly then, waking all his own gunhawks, and telling the others he was going on a scout. Glinton's body had been found in the corral at first light, and pebbles on the veranda stoop below Bennett's window had helped Justin to reconstruct what had happened.

'The theory is,' Justin added, 'that he's been working with Speakman all the time. If he hasn't, he will certainly join up with him now.'

'That's more than a theory, that's fact,' Frome said. He told his story, he told of what he had heard from Dirk and Harry Breslow; and what Blacky Breslow had told him of the Bennett-Speakman meeting months before in Kansas City.

Justin considered that. 'Sure are a cold-blooded bunch, aren't they, knocking off their own people to start a fake war? The important thing now is what do we do: do we wait for the bunch of them to come at us, or do we go after them and stomp them in the hills?'

Frome said, 'How many men have they got?'

Justin said, 'About twenty each. All are gun-experts.' He looked around at some of the men forming his own posse – the barber Ott Dakers, the boy Al Gulick, and other citizens like them. The spirit and guts might be there, but the experience and cunning would be missing.

'How many men can we muster?' Frome asked.

'Sixty to seventy. About half are cowpunchers; the rest townees. I've sent for Keester at Denton to come join us with the biggest posse he can form. But that'll take time.'

'What about the miners,' Frome said, 'there's more than five hundred of them? What happens if Speakman arms them?'

Justin smiled. 'I told you George Broome was a good friend of mine. I told you he was willing to compromise. He's gone to see the miners, tell them the true facts. They'll listen to him. They know Broome, and Speakman's only a name back east to them. Broome can guarantee that they won't back Speakman in this, providing of course, he gets to them in time to have his say. He can't guarantee that they'll side us in this, though.'

'All he need tell them is that Speakman and Bennett engineered the lynching of Tony Wolf,' Frome said.

'Oh, he'll tell them that. But that doesn't mean they'll openly fight Speakman. He's still their boss.'

Frome noticed that most of Justin's men were still in the saddle. He said, 'Why don't you fellows get some sense and

127

go to the cookshack, dry yourselves and get some coffee?'

Justin said, 'There isn't time for that. We just came this way to see if your place was still standing and if you were hereabouts. Any time now, Bennett's bunch are going to ride from them hills and stomp on ranches one by one. We're gathering at the Double Star. As soon as the broncs are rested we'll ride. You'd better come with us.'

Frome remembered Curly. He recalled the shock they had both received over the watch. He turned to look for her. She was on the other side of the room, her back to him, looking from the window.

'I've got a few plans laid out, Dave,' Justin said. 'I'd like to discuss them with you. Men are out trying to trace Bennett and Speakman's men. The sooner we hit them the better.'

Frome said, 'That idea's sound. Let's get back to the Double Star headquarters and look it over. How's Hesta taking the death of her father?'

'She's holding up bravely. She's got too much to do to mourn. She's organising things like a soldier.'

Frome nodded. 'She'll make a good rancher, Sam.' He looked to Curly again. He lowered his voice. 'I would like Curly to get back to town, Sam. Perhaps you can leave a couple of men to escort her?'

Justin nodded. 'I'll select 'em. Got a few messages I want to send to Plattsville anyway.'

Frome went to the bedroom, got a long slicker from a cupboard, opened a box of Colt cartridges and began to fill his belt. Then, pushing a cardboard box of carbine bullets into his pocket, he went back to the big room. Curly was still looking away from him. He pushed through the men talking before the door and found Justin on the

128

veranda instructing the two men he had picked to escort Curly back to Plattsville.

Justin looked up sharply as Frome pulled on his slicker. 'Where are you going, Dave?'

Frome couldn't bear to face Curly again. Not now. 'Why, with you. What are we waiting for?' He crossed to the corral and swung into the saddle of one of the horses there. He booted the Winchester and swung the bronc. He waited with the rain lashing down at him. Justin and the others mounted. Frome looked back once as they swung out of the yard, but only the two men left as Curly's escort stood on the veranda. Curly hadn't come to the door to see him ride away.

They galloped across sodden prairies, the rain hitting them head on. It trickled down their faces, and it found cracks in their slickers and sneaked down their shirt collars.

'Who'd be a cowboy?' a townee jeered. Nobody answered him. The thunderheads moved away for a time, showing the moon against a cushion of twinkling stars. Shadows about them took on substance in the light, became trees, brush, rock. They moved through cattle which stood stiff-legged and mournful in the tall wet grass and mud.

When they topped the hill above the Double Star headquarters, the thunderheads had rolled across the sky again, low above the gaunt cottonwoods, junipers and pine. The rain bounced at them and they made the descent in darkness.

Lights from ranch, bunkhouse and barns welcomed them as they swung in around the corrals. Men came from the buildings to meet them. Justin called, before dismounting, 'Any news yet?'

The reply was in the negative. Frome and Justin hitched their broncs at the same pole. Justin said, 'Something happen between you and Curly?'

Frome said, 'What makes you ask?'

'The way you heeled off. Still holding out on me, huh? A fine pal. But I soon got all the facts, didn't I?'

Frome answered dryly, 'Then there was no need for me to tell you.'

Justin laughed. 'It's a good job we're pals, Dave.'

Men moved over to greet them. Frome could see they were in good morale by the way they joked with the sheriff.

'First time I've seen the sheriff this early since election day,' somebody said. Another chipped in, 'After this, he'll want us to back him for governor.'

Justin answered, 'If you boys fight as well as you wisecrack, then I'll allow you to vote for me when the elections come along.'

Frome moved across to the ranchhouse. He was on the stoop removing his slicker when Hesta appeared at the door. She came out, closing the door and cutting the light from there. Frome noticed that she was wearing a black lace blouse and dark grey skirt. Her face was without cosmetics.

Her hand touched his arm a moment. 'How are you, Dave?'

Frome answered her whisper with a whisper. 'Fine, Hesta, just fine.' He paused. 'I was sorry to hear about Glinton.'

Justin came across to the veranda, Hesta opened the door, and they went into the long room.

More than a dozen of the smaller ranchers and town

prominents were gathered there. Frome greeted them, and Hesta left for the kitchen.

They found seats and were busy discussing the chances of finishing off Bennett and Speakman without outside help from the State, when Hesta and a maid brought them food. They were busy tucking into eggs and bacon when a Double Star rider galloped into the yard, swung from his spent bronc, and hurried into the house. He went straight to Justin, and announced that he had found the camp of the Bennett-Speakman group.

He had tracked them to Muleshoe Canyon Pass, and had seen many campfires burning in the brush-covered slopes. All the signs, he said, pointed to the use of the left slope as a more or less permanent camp.

Justin looked at the faces around them. 'Right. Do we hit them in the Pass, or don't we?'

'We hit 'em,' Frome said.

One of the ranchers raised a doubt. 'If they're on that left slope, then they've picked a good position to defend themselves. We could lose a lot of men hitting them there.'

Frome said, 'The sooner we get there, the least they'll expect us. I doubt if they'd be expecting attack for some time yet. Knowing Kyle's mind, I'd say he's pretty contemptuous of folk round here.' Frome smiled. 'He finds – or did find – most of us too slow.'

Justin said, 'I think we should hit them right now. Anybody disagree with that? We'll leave twenty men here, then hit Muleshoe Canyon Pass with every other gun we can muster.'

There was a silence as Justin looked from face to face. The only sound was the beat of the rain on windows and

131

roof. Dawn was a dirty grey blotter across the sky.

All the men nodded agreement with Justin. He got up, tugging at his shellbelt. 'We ride in an hour, then!'

CHAPTER 17

Pale streamers of the sun slanted through holes in the low-hanging clouds as Frome and Justin, at the head of fifty riders, came to a stop on the prairie two miles out from Muleshoe Canyon Pass, which towered like a fortress through the rain.

Justin cuffed the wet from his face with his sleeves. 'Seems very quiet and deserted, Dave.'

Frome saw the worry lining the sheriff's face. 'You think some kind of trap maybe?'

Justin shrugged. 'I'd hate to be the lawman in charge of a fifty-man posse which rode into a trap and were massacred. We ought to scout a little. Send five or ten men in.'

Frome lifted in his saddle, resettled himself. 'Where will that get us? We know they're there, we've seen their fire smoke. If they're setting a trap, they won't open fire on five or six or even ten men. They'll wait until they bottle the whole bunch.'

'Then what do you suggest?'

Frome said, 'I know the Pass. There's nice tall grass in there and rocks at points right up to the left slope. What I suggest is that ten men – the best riflemen – go in first, sneak in, and get settled in cover. When the main party come in, they can sweep the slope with combined carbine fire.'

'But say they don't get in without being spotted?'

'Then the main party'll have to come in and support them.'

'Just like they do it in the army, huh? OK, I'll go for that.'

Frome said, 'I'll lead the sharpshooters.'

Justin said, 'Now – wait a moment! I'm leading this party . . . I'm the law . . . I've got to do that kind of chore myself.'

Frome said, 'You're needed back here to lead in the main bunch.' He grinned. 'They'd be demoralized if you got killed. They need a fine, upright peace officer who's a born leader to command them.'

'Soft soap'll get you nowhere,' Justin said. 'But, OK, you can lead. A quarter of an hour after you've entered the Pass, I'll lead a charge in.'

'Just like they do it in the army, huh?'

'Just like it,' said the sheriff. 'Come to think of it, Dave, I think you've got the best part of the bargain. You'll go in there on your belly with plenty of cover. I'll go in leading a horse charge, right up front, with some forty carbines blazing at me. . . .'

Frome said, 'But I'm needed in there. I'm a crack shot.'

Justin pulled a mock frown. 'That's what I thought. I'll select the best shots.' He swung his horse, moving down the line, and called out nine of the men. When he had grouped them to the right, he explained the plan.

They started moving with Frome in the lead. Justin

called after Frome, 'And no goddamned heroics, Dave.'

Frome answered, 'I'll watch it.'

'Slightest sign of things going sour, you turn tail fast.'

Frome grinned. 'Slightest sign of real trouble, and Kyle won't see my rump for dust.'

Frome moved his bunch at a canter across the grass-lands, turning towards the timbered slope that led eventually to the mouth of the Pass. The riders bunched up around him, nine men who looked alike in shapeless slickers, rain-sodden hats, and wet and bearded faces. Each hefted a carbine on his knee, and each had earned a county-wide reputation for using it effectively.

They neared the slope, raking its timber with suspicious eyes. The grass was sodden beneath their ponies, and occasionally a bronc slid down in the mud. They began to climb up the slope, branches clawing at them and cascading them with water. They watched the rim, too, in case Bennett had placed a lookout this far from camp, but if he had he had not so far shown himself.

Halfway up the slope they turned their ponies, moving in Indian file along it to the mouth of the Pass. Long minutes later, they were within sight of the drop away which made the mouth of the Pass. They dismounted and tied their ponies to the brush. They grouped around Frome for last minute instructions. Frome told them that if things became too hot they would have to cross the canyon and work their way out in the brush. Since there was plenty of cover, he added, that should not be too difficult.

Carbines raised, they slipped and skidded down the slope and moved in a crouch for the mouth of the Pass. A mile and a half away, little dots above the grass, the posse

135

sat and waited and watched. They went through the drenched grass, heads down, and moved in between the towering sides. The grass was high around them, concealing all but their faces. Then the slopes on either side fell away, fire smoke wafted from the mouths of caves in the timbered slopes. Nothing – nobody – moved up there.

Now they fanned out, rustling through the grass, boots coated in mud, faces glistening with the wet that shook from the grass tops. Frome moved in a duck-like crouch, knees almost together, feet splayed out. Fine crystals of water bounced on his face and hands and burst. His grip on his carbine was slippery. The cold dampness seemed to reach every part of him.

Halfway to his objective, a cluster of rocks just out from the slope, he looked for signs of a possible planned ambush. He watched the slope behind him, but there was no sign of movement there. He looked and listened for horses picketed close at hand, for if Kyle was setting an ambush, he would need ponies to hit them from the sides. He neither saw nor heard horses nearby.

He was almost at his objective when he saw the first movement on the slope. A man appeared at the mouth of a cave, stretching his arms and yawning. The man gave every appearance of having just been asleep. If Kyle was laying an ambush, Frome reflected, then he was certainly going in for stage effects.

Then Frome ran into difficulties. The ground rose in front of him, but the grass remained at the same height. He had reached a slight rise, and it put him head and shoulders above the grass. He quickly dropped and guessed that several other men would have to do the same.

He found himself bellying through a pea-green world of slime and mud and smell. It was stifling. The greasy mass seemed to beat in on him as if to suffocate him. He raised his head every yard to suck in air and scrutinize the slope. The minutes dragged by. It seemed like ages since he had flopped down. He began to worry about the time . . . wondering if he would be in place before Justin struck.

The sweat ran from him and mixed with the rain. He began to take less care, dragging down the stalks to clear a passage. Then suddenly the colour scheme ahead of him changed, suddenly he was there as a grey mass appeared a yard in front of him. He had reached the rocks. He moved ahead swiftly now. He came up the face of the rock, breathing heavily and rested against them. A slight scurrying in the grass a few feet from him, and a boy in a rain-glossened slicker pulled himself free, his tongue licking at his lips.

Frome recognized him as one of the sharpshooters selected by Justin, but didn't know his name. He took his place beside Frome without speaking, wiping the wet from a Spencer seven-shot with a neckerchief. When he had finished, he said, 'Can't be no fun being a worm, Mister Frome.'

Frome didn't reply. He had taken a tip from the youngster and, with a neckerchief, was wiping some of the wet from his rifle. He looked up the slope while working. He undid his slicker, opening it wide, broke open the box of carbine bullets and let them fall loose in his pocket.

As he finished, he heard the distant beat of hoofs. An excitement gripped him. And the youth. They leaned forward on the rocks. They poked their carbines over the rim, pointing up the slope. And they waited.

The hoofbeats became louder. Suddenly they were like the roll of thunder. Still no movement on the slope. Frome lived an anxious moment. Then he realized the rain and the cold would have driven Bennett's men deep into the caves ... but there should be a lookout ... somewhere.

And then came the bark of a carbine. Three times the carbine roared. The echo of the shots clattered across the canyon. Frome raked the slope looking for the tell-tale smoke from the sentry's rifle. But the nearest he got to it was smoke snatching high above a cluster of cottonwoods near to the canyon's rim.

He had to forget the sentry as men came spilling from the mouths of the caves, men with carbines, slipping and diving for cover in the brush. Frome's rifle stock slapped his shoulder. He aimed on a man and squeezed. Other shots rattled out along the grass around him. The sound hung sluggishly on the damp air. Frome jerked the guard, swinging the rifle, pressing the trigger on another target. A man took his slug in the head as he stood poised in a cave mouth. Frome's movements became mechanical. He worked the guard and then he fired, pumping slugs up the slope at second intervals. Another hit sent a man spilling from a narrow ledge clutching a smashed elbow. A third went head over heels as Frome's slug punched his legs from beneath him, folding him into brush.

One glance along the slope showed Frome that the rest of the men were scoring. He saw several desperadoes folding or spinning from the ledges, dead or wounded. But now he was slowing; now he had to search for his targets as Bennett's men gained cover. And now slugs began to whip towards him. And behind him, their horses hoofs now muffled by the thick grass, Justin brought the posse in at a gallop, with bullets ripping amongst them.

A bullet scythed a runnel in the grass inches from Frome's head. Instinctively he lifted his head and saw the breeze waft gunsmoke from the cottonwoods. Guessing that the man might be in the branches of the tallest tree, Frome swung his rifle that way, and pumped four shells into its branches. A moment later a man, still clutching a carbine, fell eight-foot to the ground, rolled off a ledge and crashed some twenty feet down the slope.

Frome lowered his aim, pumping the rest of his shots into the thickets just beneath the cave mouths above which gunsmoke was clouding. Then he found his carbine empty. He swung, jacking home fresh shells, and looked across the basin as he did so.

He saw Justin, low in the saddle, and he saw the rest of the posse fanned out behind him. He saw two riderless horses. He saw a pony go down and throw a rider heavily. He saw a Double Star puncher clutch at his face as he was kicked backwards off his pony by a high calibre rifle bullet. As he swung to pump more shells up the slope, he saw two ponies, almost level with him, go down and throw their riders. The two riders, however, came scrambling through the grass to join them, rifles ready in their hands. With the reinforcements, with four rifles behind the rocks, Frome instructed the men to keep firing into the brush, and not to wait until they sighted targets. The men responded. Four carbines spattered flame, covering the brush below the caves with a stream of lead.

More rifles joined in the battle. A minute later, re-loading his rifle with sweat-slippery fingers, Frome saw that more of the posse had dismounted now. Some had shot their ponies and were using them as barriers. Some were down behind rocks or just bellying down in grass. Something like forty carbines were sending lead among Bennett and Speakman's crew.

Frome decided it was time to move. He slapped the shoulder of the youth beside him. He thumbed towards the slope, and then he moved. He shafted down into the tall grass beyond the rock formation, and the youth dropped at his heels. He began to belly through the grass. The earth was alive with sounds. The drum of hoofs echoed up at him as spooked ponies raced and curved across the battleground.

The youth came up beside Frome and smiled. They began to climb upwards as the slope began. Then suddenly the youth was jerking on Frome's sleeve and pointing. Frome couldn't hear what the boy was saying above the din of battle, but he saw that he was scared. Turning, then, he saw the horsemen. Three men, bunched in half a dozen horses, were coming down from timber on the slope at a mad speed, trying to break out from the trap.

Frome slapped his rifle to his shoulder, fired, and a pony went down. The kid fired and a man was smacked from his saddle. Frome fired and dropped the next man. The ponies swerved sharply, turning, ignoring the rein. The third man had disappeared when the dust kicked up by the crashing horse-hoofs had cleared.

They made no attempt to hide now from the men on the slopes. With the brush only some ten yards ahead, Frome decided to run for it. He raced forward with the youth hard behind him. Bullets savaged the ground around them. Then they were hidden from the men on

140

the slope by the jutting overhang of the brush. They hit the muddy wall. Frome looked up into the tangled mass, looking for a way through. Finally he found what appeared to be a narrow water washout. He sprang up, clawing at brush, the mud caking up beneath his slipping boots. He got a firm grip, placed legs over a stumpy pine, and, bending, dragged the youth up.

Then he bellied down and began to push through the darkness under the brush. Mud and slime sucked at him. His carbine was slippery with it. They wormed on, moving fast. Frome saw daylight in the foliage a dozen yards ahead, clawing towards it, using branches as a hold. The ground climbed steeply. He was sweating when he reached it. Propping his legs against a gnarled root, he heaved the boy on to the ledge beside him. He poked his head carefully into the open. Behind a felled pine twenty feet to his left, he saw a Bennett man pumping shots down into the basin. He worked the brush open that way by lifting it with his rifle. Propping it up, he whispered to the boy, 'Get him.'

Pale of face, the boy levelled and fired; the man toppled forward over the rim.

They went on again, following the ridge of the washout, worming beneath more brush. Occasionally they heard movement close at hand, just beyond the thickets. They passed the blood-stained body of a sharpshooter, topped from the rim above earlier in the battle. Further on, somewhere to their right, a man called out in a pain-choked voice for water.

They came into the open again, looked right, and saw the caves below them. Finding cover, they looked down, and saw men secreted in the brush. They began together, poking carbines over the rim, pumping shots at the exposed men, killing some, wounding others, and sending them, demoralised, for further shelter in the brush.

Frome could see the wide basin now. He could see the scattered posse-men. Even as he looked, several men came running for the slope, pumping the triggers on their rifles as they moved. He knew now that it was all over, that they were on the point of defeating Bennett and Speakman. But he still had to find Bennett. And Speakman. Telling the youth to stay in position and fire down into the slope, Frome moved upwards. He had to turn to his left and again to his left as the slope wall became too steep. It took him from the scene of the battle, but he hurried on, sure that if Bennett would be anywhere it would be on the rimrock.

He rounded an outcropping and came up a track that snaked to the rim of the canyon. He began to move up it, gripping grass and bush as leverage to make better speed on the slippery track.

He was halfway up, bellied down, using his left hand as a hold, when two men appeared on the rim. They dropped to the track, moving quickly, and for a fraction of a second, they didn't see Frome. He had enough time to lift his carbine. As he pressed the trigger on the leader, they saw him. The man he hit rolled down the slope, his feet barely missing the rancher. The other, squatting, already sliding, clawed for his holstered gun.

Frome jacked the guard, pressed on the man, and found that the carbine was empty. He dropped it, and his hand dived for his holstered Colt. He had to drag his slicker away. The man fired, but his shooting was wild. Mud churned up by Frome's head. Another bullet skidded and ripped past his feet. The man was still sliding, crashing nearer to him, still pumping shells.

Frome's Colt came up, taking aim from his static position. He saw the man now, scared, almost on top of him. The man's mouth opened wide, yelling either for help or mercy. Frome, jerking the trigger, placed two bullets there, aiming for the cavern-like mouth.

The man thundered forward, rolling over Frome, heavy riding boots slapping the rancher in the mouth and bringing the salty taste of blood there. Without looking back at the rolling man, Frome sprang up, clawing again for the rim.

He reached it, folded over it. A man was halfway across the top, carbine at his side, racing for this same track. It took him a moment to recognize Frome. And then he fired, the slug scorching off the rim, showering Frome with rocky splinters. Frome fired with his Colt and missed the dancing figure. A bullet slammed across his shoulder, ripping open his slicker. Frome levelled his Colt, holding grimly to the slippery surface with his palm extended left hand, digging his fingers into the mushy ground. He fired one, and the man staggered. He fired twice more, pumping his shots into the man. The rifle dropped, the man's head shafted skyward, then he crumbled to the ground.

Frome swung on to the rim, got to his feet and began to move toward the right where rock formation broke the flat surface. He kept inward from the rim so as not to be fired upon by the posse.

He reached a boulder stand, rounded it, and came up near a man. The man was tall, dressed in a slicker. A Spencer seven-shot was aimed downward, and as Frome saw him, so the man fired.

The man swung then to jack home a fresh shell, and then he saw Frome. It was Peter Speakman. Frome fired his Colt from his hip, but Speakman was sliding to one side, his knee folding. Frome darted at the mine operator, pumped the Colt's trigger, only to hear an ominous click. His Colt was empty.

He saw the tight sneer on Speakman's face. He saw the Spencer, with a fresh shell in the barrel, coming up. Then Frome launched himself.

CHAPTER 18

Speakman's carbine levelled. Frome had a horrible sensation that he wouldn't reach him in time. The Spencer was almost pointed at Frome's chest as his boots skated over the smooth rock surface. His Colt cracked against the barrel of Speakman's gun with a metallic clang, turning it as the man fired. The bullet slammed at rock yards away. Then, sweeping the Colt onward, Frome laid the barrel along the mine operator's head, putting all the power into his arm that he could muster. Frome lost balance then, skidding to the ground, sprawling, pain zipping through him.

Speakman teetered back, dropped his rifle. Then he was on the edge of the rim, his arms slicing air trying to regain balance. His mouth was a scarlet O as he fell away, over the side of the canyon rim, and a horrible scream whipped back at Frome, bringing his heart into his mouth.

Then Frome was up and moving again, clawing up Speakman's rifle, jerking a shell into the breech, hurrying along the rim. A man twisted up from the rocks at him.

Frome brought the stock round, slammed it into the man's surprised face, dropping him unconscious.

Looking quickly down the slope, he saw that the battle was almost over on the lower slopes. He saw Justin way back in the grass, his coat off, somebody bandaging his arm. He saw a line of men advancing up the slope. He saw other scattered figures rounding up the ponies.

But where was Bennett? Surely not on the slope somewhere? If Speakman had been up here, then surely Kyle Bennett had been with him, since it seemed logical that they would be together? Frome moved on again, impatience building within him.

Then he remembered how he had seen men fleeing from the battle. Could Bennett have decided to make his escape after seeing that the battle was lost? It seemed probable. Speakman, with more to lose, would have hung on those few extra minutes in a desperate bid to save his vast copper empire. But Bennett would have scurried away. But where? Then, recalling earlier visits to the canyon, Frome turned hard left, moving inward across the rim, guessing where the Bennett-Speakman gang would have kept their ponies.

Before he had reached the other side of the wall, he heard the sound of hoofs. He began to run, raising the carbine. Near the edge, he dropped and crawled forward. Looking down on the inner canyon, an apron of tree-studded rock and grass, he saw four riders, strung out in a line, swinging up the opposite side towards a crevice in the canyon face. The leader was Kyle Bennett.

They were two hundred yards away. Frome felt frustration grip him. Surely Kyle Bennett, out in the lead, wasn't going to get away. Not after all this. He had to get a

146

horse and follow. He looked around the basin for the remuda. He saw forty-odd saddled ponies moving along the basin, bunched, probably driven that way by Bennett. He realized that before he could reach them they would be more than a mile away, if not out of the inner canyon into the main one.

Frome swung his carbine towards the four men. He had to get a horse. He aimed carefully, levelling on the last of the four men as the leader disappeared into the crevice. Frome squeezed the trigger. At the end of his barrel he saw the man shudder, slide limply from the saddle, and the pony turn, spooked. The two riders still showing did not look back. Spurring their broncs they dashed at the crevice, both fighting to get to its cover first. They disappeared, and Frome was already moving, his eyes on the pony which had turned away. He had guessed right. The pony had not tried to escape by galloping for the crevice because it was blocked by the mounted men. It turned downward, moving at a canter for the canyon floor.

Frome poked his legs over the rim, abandoning Speakman's rifle because he could see a carbine in the saddle bucket of the riderless pony. He lowered himself to a shelf, clawed along it, dropped to another ledge, and moved along that. His hands and face were mud-caked and mixed with his own sweat. His clothes were torn. He abandoned his ripped slicker to make better speed.

Halfway down the slope, he saw that the fall-away was not too abrupt. Folding off the ledge, he skidded down the slope, using his hands and feet as a brake. He wormed through brush and finally reached the canyon floor. Breaking out of timber he saw the pony, a sorrel, standing by a muddy pool in the canyon's centre. He moved towards it casually, whistling softly.

The animal, still spooky, watched Frome, but did not turn from him. Frome reached it, gathered up the reins and stepped into the saddle as he swung it. He heeled it up the slope for the narrow gorge through which Bennett had escaped. He took the rifle from the bucket, and inspected it.

It was new, probably one of those purchased by Glinton and brought from Gulick's by Bennett. Frome found that the carbine was empty. So he refilled it with slugs from his shirt pocket.

He reached the crevice and found that it was a narrow cut some six foot wide. He remembered it of old, a narrow alley of towering rocks which led to rocky wastelands, to pasture and eventually, to Plattsville.

He put the pony into the pass, his senses tuned for movement ahead. He didn't think that Bennett would plan a bushwack, for Bennett couldn't have known that it was Frome who had fired the shot or had made any attempt yet to follow. Bennett would be on the run. He would want to cover ground fast. He would make all possible speed for the border.

With these thoughts, but remaining alert, Frome put the bronc at full speed through the gorge. The sharp crack of his pony's hoofs sounded like thunder off the rock walls and floor. He found that after a quarter of a mile the ground widened, and he could put the pony into a lope. Then the gorge fizzled out into a half basin, dropping to a brush-choked floor with narrow trails made by cattle. When he was well into the floor, he bent several times from his saddle, looking for Bennett's sign.

Eventually he found prints, but where he least expected them. Instead of turning for the wastelands Bennett had apparently turned towards Plattsville. Frome followed. He came out of the brush to open ground, and the signs still moved westward toward Plattsville. Now the sign was easy to follow, and he put the bronc forward at speed. Broken branches en route told him with what speed Bennett had moved this way.

He followed sign for three miles through brush country, the sign still pointing to town. He decided that Bennett had turned that way to outfox any pursuit, that he would cut away suddenly somewhere before town. Bennett would be hoping that the posse, agreeing that he was going to Plattsville, wouldn't bother to follow tracks too carefully, and would continue towards the town long after he had turned away.

The miles chipped away. Noon passed. The thunderheads rolled across the sky, cutting off the few streamers of sun which had poked down. It began to rain, and without the slicker, Frome became soaked and cold.

He traversed high ground, prairie and a tangled forest, still following trail. Occasionally he checked that the three horses had gone this way, wanting to make sure that Bennett hadn't turned off and left his men to confuse pursuit.

Towards evening he reached the Tulle River. He smiled grimly. This was where Bennett would pull his trick. He would turn either up stream or down and, unless he picked the right way, Frome would lose valuable hours.

He put the pony into the water, crossing straight, looking for prints on the opposite bank which he thought wouldn't be there. To his surprise, he found that three

149

horses – the very three he had followed – had waded ashore and struck out directly for the town. Frome, still puzzled, put his horse into a mile-eating gallop, wondering why Bennett would head for Plattsville.

CHAPTER 19

Old Man Night had pumped lavish helpings of his indigo dye into the thunderclouds and Frome forded the Plattsville Creek in rain and darkness and saw the lights of the town twinkling below him. He looked at the sprawl of the town, from the railhead at one end to the skeletal sun-sucked clapboards at the other. Things seemed normal. No gunfire. The only sound the distant tinkle of a saloon piano. If Bennett was in town, the few able-bodied citizens who hadn't joined one of the posses didn't know about it.

Frome put the bronc downhill, swinging across pasture which was as sodden and oozy as his own clothes. He thought of Bennett and what would have brought the man to town. He thought he knew. The town was practically wide open, all the lawmen and best citizens were up at the Muleshoe Canyon Pass, and it wasn't like Bennett to slink away with his tail between his legs, conceding defeat. Now Bennett's ego would demand that he left his mark, that he rode out in triumph. Moreover, that he rode away with sufficient funds.

Well, there were funds at the bank, and nobody much to look after them. An urgent call to the chief clerk, a gun barrel jabbed in the man's back, a walk through the deserted alleys to the bank on Main, a few moments for the clerk to open the safe. . . . Frome saw it all, and it was the way Bennett would work it. You don't know a man for six years without being able to predict some of his moves and his way of thinking.

Frome put his pony into a sprawl of alleys at the centre of the town. Occasional light dripped from shack windows. He swung left, then right, and came to the rear of The Drovers. Curly was in there, somewhere, near at hand, and it brought back the scene at his cabin, and an ache touched him.

He swung the pony to a wall, hitched it at a post, then slid from the saddle. He headed for the back door of the saloon, found it unlocked and entered it. He moved along the dark corridor. Light shafted from beneath the door to Sturmer's office. He knuckled the door, and Mike Sturmer's voice reached him, telling him to come in.

He entered. Mike Sturmer, still wearing his bar apron, was seated behind his desk, knife and fork in hand, about to slice into a porterhouse steak. It reminded Frome that he was hungry. The aroma of fried onions greeted him.

Sturmer looked him up and down. He was surprised.

'Dave, what a surprise,' he said.

Frome crossed to the table. 'Curly get back OK?'

'Yeah, Dave. About Curly. . . .'

'Seen Bennett?'

'Bennett? You mean – here – in town?'

Frome nodded. Sturmer put down his knife and fork. 'No, what's happened?'

Frome picked up the fork, stabbed it at a section of steak, and lifted it to his mouth. 'Speakman's dead. We've

defeated their mob at Muleshoe Canyon Pass. Bennett got
away . . . headed this way.'

'You mean you've wiped out the entire bunch?'

Frome chewed on the steak. 'Huh. Good steak.' He
scooped up some onion, popped it into his mouth. 'Order
me one of these, Mike.' He moved to the door.

Sturmer came up. 'Sure. You need it. But where're you
going?'

'Over to the bank.'

'This time of night?'

But Frome had gone. He moved along the alley,
reached Main. It was still raining and the street was
deserted. He looked up towards the sheriff's office. It was
in darkness. His eyes moved to the bank. No light from
there either. He smiled. Bennett had it all his own way. He
had to be right. Bennett wouldn't miss something as easy
as this. And he had help – two gunslicks.

He figured as he crossed Main that Bennett couldn't
have been more than an hour ahead of him. He reached
the opposite boardwalk, cut down into an alley beside Ma
Connick's, and reached the rear. He pictured what
Bennett would have to do on reaching town. First he
would have to find or buy fresh horses. He would need to
have them hitched at the rear of the bank. Then he would
have to go a half a mile to the chief clerk's house, bring
him back, and yet keep off the main street.

Perhaps the gunhawks with him could move about
openly. But Bennett couldn't. He was too well known, and
everybody would have heard by now that he was behind
the murders of Denny Le Roy, Glinton Le Roy, Matt Grape
and Dwight Taber. The miners in town wouldn't shake his
hand on meeting him either – not if Broome had told

them that Bennett had lynched Tony Wolf.

He passed behind the café building, the sounds and smells of cooking reached him. It reminded him of when he had last eaten – at the Double Star at dawn that day. Hesta had cooked him eggs and bacon, fresh rolls and coffee. He thought of Hesta, remembered that she had been without the engagement ring that morning. He remembered shaking her hand before they had ridden out. Her words imprinted themselves on his mind.

'Take care of yourself, Dave,' she had whispered. 'I was wrong about you – terribly wrong – but it's too late now.' There had been something final about the way she had said goodbye. She had not needed to use that expression. She could have said 'so long', or 'I'll see you soon,' but she had said 'goodbye, Dave.'

The alley opened suddenly before him. He saw the black poles of an old corral rear suddenly in the faint light thrown from a shack window further down the alley. He was at the rear of the bank now, and he lifted the carbine.

Now he listened for sounds. He heard nothing. He moved on again, reaching the side entrance to the bank. Then he heard a horse stomp the hard-baked ground near the corral. He swung. Beyond the corral, at the other side, he saw the blurred lines of three ponies. And a rider. A man was astride the middle pony. A footstep somewhere in the bank made a board creak.

Frome moved away from the building, darting around the corral, moving swiftly yet quietly. He came up around the man, saw that he was unhitching the ponies. Even as Frome moved forward, the carbine reversed to strike, the man swung the ponies from the rail and moved for the bank building.

154

Bennett was doing it by the clock. The man would have allowed Bennett and his companion some ten minutes in the bank, and then moved to the backdoor with the fresh getaway ponies. The hoofbeats of the ponies allowed Frome to follow the man. He stepped quickly between the ponies. He swung the carbine's stock. It hit the man on the side of the head with a sound like a cleaver going through a hunk of beef. Frome dropped the rifle, grabbed for the horses to pacify them. The man slid limply from the saddle without a sound. Frome stepped into his place.

The horses settled and moved forward for the bank building.

Frome stopped the ponies at the rear door, his Colt held low by his side. He looked up the alley, saw the lights on Main. Anybody passing, looking down and seeing the ponies with a rider in the saddle at the rear door of the bank, would certainly give the alarm. If he had the courage, he might start firing.

A minute passed. Then footsteps inside the bank building. They were fast. The bolt rattled on the door and it swung open. A pencil of light seeped down a crack. Then two figures filled the doorway. Each carried money sacks.

Frome brought the gun up, levelled it as the men stepped into the open, and said, 'Kyle?' Then he fired at the first figure, not giving the man time to go for his holstered gun. The man folded away. But the second man was already moving, launching himself at the nearest of the ponies.

Frome heard his snarl and recognized him as Kyle Bennett. A coin bag struck the animal's rump. Then Bennett brought up his boot at its stomach. And then he ducked away.

The horse came up on its hind legs, rolling away, bumping into Frome's bronc. The pony on Frome's right broke away, galloping for the mouth of the alley. The injured bronc followed it; and Frome's, skidding and bucking and trying to unseat him, attempted to follow the others.

Frome sprang from the saddle, relaxing his body. He hit the ground and rolled away. He heard Bennett running . . . running down towards the corral. He balled over, snatching his other Colt from his holster, not attempting to find the one he had dropped. He aimed it along the alley and fired at a vague shape.

The shape vanished near the poles. Frome came up in a crouch. He went to the side of the alley, working along to the disused corral. He heard voices now and movement on Main Street. People were hurrying to see what had happened, but Frome knew that they would not come too close. They would stay at the top of the alley until the gunfight ended and make things difficult for him by creating a lot of noise.

If Bennett was making any noise then Frome didn't hear it. He could only rely upon his eyes, and there was little light. For all he knew Bennett could have ducked around the corral and be well away by now. The end of the bank building fell away and Frome was in the open. Vaguely, in the light from that one lamp further down, he could see the flaked, weather eroded poles of the corral. He stepped out and towards it instinctively sensing in some way that Bennett had not gone far . . . that he was somewhere near the corral.

Then flame stabbed across the corral towards him. He

ducked. The bullet gouged wood behind him. Even as he ducked away, so Frome fired, pumping a shot across the corral.

Flame answered him, from a yard away as Bennett moved and fired. Frome spread his legs. Aimed the Colt across the corral, then began to fan the trigger and move the sight. He pumped four bullets across the corral at spaced intervals of a yard. Then he collapsed on to his knees, fingers snatching fresh slugs from his shellbelt and reloading the Colt.

A long silence. Frome watched between the poles. Then Bennett's voice reached him. A chuckle . . . or a sob? It seemed to end on a note of hysteria, or fear, or pain.

Frome strained his eyes, the Colt, reloaded, coming up.

Bennett spoke again, an unmistakable sneer in his voice. 'What are you waiting for, gun-shy?'

Frome knew better than to answer him. He began to belly forward, sliding beneath the pole, worming to the centre of the corral.

'You've blocked every move I've made, Frome,' Bennett said a moment later, 'but I'll take you with me . . . they won't get me to hang.'

Frome still didn't reply. He thought he had placed Bennett now. There was an old lean-to wall parallel with the corral. Frome judged it to be eight foot high and some five yards long. Somewhere along it, probably propped against it, hidden by it, Bennett stood and waited.

'I underestimated you, Frome. Thought you a no-gun. Shouldn't have sent the Breslows . . . should've come for you myself. I didn't get you then, but I'll live long enough to get you now.'

Frome reached the corral poles. The wall began some

ten feet away. He raised himself, laying the barrel on the pole, waiting. He couldn't open fire before Bennett showed himself, he realized. If he tried to get Bennett by firing wildly it would be like trying to hit a needle in a haystack, and Bennett would only need to fire once to hit him.

'Well, where are you?' Bennett jeered. A slight movement. 'Waiting for your sheriff and the posse?'

Frome swung the barrel of his Colt to the right, placing Bennett at the lower part of the wall by his voice. It came to him that Bennett's voice sounded unnatural, off-key.

'I tell you,' Bennett snarled suddenly, 'you're not going to take me alive and hang me!'

And then Frome saw Bennett lunge out from the wall six feet from him, turn, and stagger towards the poles where he lay.

'I'm coming for you. . . .'

Frome fired as Bennett began to speak. He got the big man squarely in the Colt's barrel line, and he fanned the hammer, pumping all six shots at the lunging man. He saw Bennett vividly in the flashes made by the gun. He saw the big man's arms flake out. He noticed that Bennett's hands were empty as the hammer fell with a dull click on an empty cylinder.

Frome forked over the poles. He moved to where Bennet had fallen. He bent to his knees, struck a match on his boot, and looked at Bennett's hands. The righthand was wrapped in bandage. The bandage was muddy black and the blood on it was hard, dried. He noticed that there was no guns in Bennett's holsters.

The match went out. He struck another, moving along the wall. He found the bags of money. And he found

THE KANSAS FAST GUN

Bennett's Colt by the corral rail. It came to him then that Bennett had been unarmed when he had taunted and challenged him; that Bennett had stepped out purposely to his death by bullets . . . rather than surrender and await a judicial trial and a law-man's rope.

People moved in around the corral now. Lanterns were held high, chasing away the shadows.

Frome looked once more at Bennett. The man was face down, his head oddly twisted. And in the light from a lamp Frome could see the smile which twisted the blond man's lips. Bennett had a reason to smile, he reflected. He had lost out on all his earlier tricks, but the last one had paid off.

A man moved up beside Frome. He asked timidly, 'What happened?'

Frome said caustically, 'Indians tried to rob the bank.'

'Indians?' the man was surprised. 'What would Indians be doing? . . . But that's Bennett, ain't it.'

'Was – Bennett.'

Frome pushed through the crowd. He saw a man he recognized. He said, 'There's a lot of dough lying about in canvas bags. Better get some help and round it up. Also you'd better go check in the bank. I think you'll find the chief clerk out cold.'

The man began to select some help.

Frome moved down the alley towards Main. The hate had left him now. He felt sapped, deflated. He became aware of his discomfort, hunger, tiredness. He thought of the steak he had seen Sturmer slicing into. He thought of the big bath Karno had up at the hotel, he thought of Curly.

He saw a figure, slight, almost boyish, fill the mouth of

159

the alley. He quickened his step and his heartbeat seemed to increase in tempo. Then he saw that it was Curly, and that she was moving towards him . . . moving fast.

She met him near the mouth of the alley, her face lifted, fear leaving it, a radiant smile replacing it. He took her into his arms and he kissed her. She stepped back slightly and he saw the tears of joy that flaked her cheeks.

'Oh, Dave,' she whispered, 'it doesn't matter. . . . It was so long ago.'

'But. . . ?'

She touched his lips with her fingers.

'I loved him – yes,' she said, 'but that was in another lifetime.'

Frome ran his hands through her silk soft hair. Then they turned, arm in arm, and moved towards the board-walk of Main.

A P